Where is Noemi?

Leah T. Williams

Published by Leah T. Williams, 2023.

WHERE IS NOEMI?

First edition. November 1, 2023.

Copyright © 2023 Leah T. Williams.

ISBN: 978-1962776028

Written by Leah T. Williams.

"A person who strays
from home is like
a bird that strays
from its nest."
- Proverbs 27:8

Prologue

"We should start back," Stephen urged as the streets darkened around them. Hanging tree branches stretched like eerie fingers that would snatch them up at any moment and store them where lost children in a bread-crumb strewn forest were hidden away forever.

"Just a little bit further," Jasmin encouraged.

Though every familiar house, dull and unsteady, identical in size and build sported stairs leading up to a porch, Jasmin sought one that was different and she was determined to find it. They'd gotten too far now just to go back without any answers.

"Jaz," Stephen pleaded. "It's getting late." Worry filled his eyes. His eyes darted towards the nearest bus stop because he knew no Uber would ever stop on these streets. Where would he tell the driver to go anyway? He had no clue.

"She's gotta be out here, Stephen." Jasmin encouraged herself more than she did Stephen. "I just know it."

"We've been out here all afternoon," Stephen flailed his arms in protest. "And you still haven't found this house. Are you sure this is where your sister brought you?"

Jasmin ignored him and continued to squint at the little Monopoly houses: identical twins, triplets, quadruplets, and whatever came after quadruplets; she felt she was getting closer.

"That's it," Jasmin shrieked. "That's the house! She's gotta be in there."

"You sure?" Stephen questioned. To him, nothing distinguished this house. No different than the others, how could Jasmin differentiate when Stephen knew he couldn't? He observed everything, especially about Jasmin, even a fresh freckle on her face. He knew she wasn't going to give up because that's who she was, someone who never quit. But now, this, he thought, was not their job. This, he thought, was too dangerous for them both!

Jasmin quickened her step to climb each stair with unmitigated dedication. As she raised her hand to knock on the door, Stephen grabbed her wrist.

"Wait!"

"For what?" Jasmin said, annoyed.

"What if it's the wrong house?"

"What if it's the right one?" She parried.

"What if she's not in there?"

"Then," Jasmin paused, taking in the garden gnome minding his own business in his corner. She hadn't thought that far ahead. All she knew was that she needed to find her sister and find her soon. "Then we keep looking."

Then I keep looking, she said to herself. Refusing to give up hope, Jasmin yanked her arm out of Stephen's and lightly rapped on the door. With each knock, she hoped an answer she sought would pop out.

Bread Crumbs From Leftover Bread

1. Ask your parents' permission. They are still in charge of you and whatever you make.

2. Don't use ingredients that people are expecting to find when they get home. Imagine coming home to make a sandwich and there's no leftover bread because someone (you) have used it all to make a recipe. So, refer to step 1.

3. Find any bread you have in the house. it can be stale or you can use hot dog buns or English muffins, whatever.

4. Rip it into evenly sized pieces. No need to measure it; just try your best.

5. Turn the oven on to 300°F, put the bread on a tray that can take the heat, spread it out and bake it anywhere from 20 - 40 minutes.

6. Check it. If any pieces are soft, put them back in. Let the toasted bread cool.

7. Then, put it in a plastic bag, take a rolling pin or plastic hammer and hit the bag til it crumbs. If the bag breaks, wrap it in a dish towel. Do not. I repeat. Do not use a real hammer on Ma's kitchen counter.

8. Store your crumbs in a plastic bag or container. They'll last that way for about 6 months.

9. Ma likes to add some Italian seasoning. Yum!

Now

Jasmin silently wished her mother had called 911 rather than driven all the way down to the police station. *They could've come to our home*, Jasmin thought. *They make home visits, don't they?* On the T.V. shows, Jasmin watched the cops go into people's houses: they looked around, surveyed the place, asked questions, touched furniture, sat like kings of the palace, and asked more of the same questions. They wrapped yellow tape around the "crime scene" marking for everyone that something happened; a crime had been committed. Cops marked their territory like dogs peeing on their favorite fire hydrant. They consoled the victim's family all while surreptitiously searching the family's home for clues. *I hope this doesn't happen to our family,* Jasmin thought. She didn't say any of this though; she just did what she was told. *I hope Ma knows what she's doing.*

Maybe Ma didn't want all that yellow tape surrounding their house for people to pass by, stop and stare. Maybe she didn't want cars out front with bright lights or glaringly loud sirens attracting the neighbor's attention. Maybe she didn't want strangers traipsing around the house looking for God knows what. Maybe Ma was trying to avoid all of that. All these thoughts marched around in Jasmin's mind looking for some place to settle.

Neither easy nor cheap to find a parking spot, Ma's determination got them one anyway. *Who's ever heard of paying for parking at the police station?* Jasmin thought. With no pedestrians in the crosswalk, no one at the bus stop, in front of the police station, the streets seemed haunted.

Glass walls surrounded the building both Jasmin and her mother stared at, not that Jasmin had ever been to a police station before. Having avoided a visit, she thought it was a really good thing, but ironically the building that loomed in front of them did not look very police-ish. No one was rushing in and out of the police station like they did on Jasmin's shows. Lawyers weren't standing on the stairs discussing the cases. The news media wasn't outside chasing people for a comment. *Probably because there were no people*, Jasmin thought.

All of Jasmin's knowledge of the police derived from *The Flash* and Law & Order, but mostly from *The Flash* because Barry Allen worked as a forensic scientist as his cover job, when he wasn't *The Flash*. What Barry Allen actually did for a day job was a mystery to Jasmin, but even so, she admired Barry's career. When anyone asked her what she wanted to do when she grew up, she'd perk her chest up, lift her chin and proudly enunciate *a Forensic Scientist*. She didn't say this because of Barry Allen but because it sounded official and important.

Jasmin and Ma walked into a plain building, nothing like the shimmering glass wrapping on the outside, a clear contrast. *This must be where hope came to die*, Jasmin thought. Pictures in glass frames of old white men lined the walls. Name plates placed under each picture gave the name but they were not large enough for Jasmin to discern. However, she made a mental note to check out the names on her way out. As for now, she had to follow Ma because Ma was clearly on a mission.

Worry lines crowded Ma's forehead and her eyes were bloodshot. In no mood to wait on Jasmin to read names on a wall, Jasmin continued walking behind Ma ensuring she was within reach. Ma walked like she'd been at the police station before and confident in where to go and who to see.

At the end of the walkway, a woman stood behind a thick plastic screen dotted with metal holes. At least they didn't have to pick up a telephone to talk to her like in the prison scenes on T.V. *Is that only for visitors?* Jasmin wondered. *Barry Allen didn't give me much information about this. Either way, I guess the cops have to be protected too.*

Though Jasmin imagined every person in a police station wearing a uniform, this woman did not. In *The Flash* everyone wore a uniform except the detectives and the forensic scientists like Barry Allen. Instead she was wrapped like a sausage in a collared shirt with embroidered letters on her left breast that read *OPD*. *Maybe this woman was a forensic scientist or a detective since she didn't wear a uniform*, Jasmin thought.

"Can I help you?" the tightly stuffed lady asked gruffly. Her words sounded like *What do you want?* Her eyes were glued to whatever was on the desk in front of her, too busy to look in the faces of her customers. *Are we customers*? Jasmin thought. *Is that what you call people who need the help of the police, customers?*

"My little girl is missing!" the words were hazy as they left Ma's mouth but they were clear enough to jolt the woman from her trance. She looked up as the words "LITTLE, GIRL" and "MISSING" left Ma's lips. Jasmin wanted to laugh at the words "little girl" but not "missing" because *missing* was serious. Missing shoe lace. Missing sock. Anything *missing* needed to be found, especially a human. But, Noemi hadn't been a "little girl" in a long time. Jasmin didn't say this out loud, and hopefully the expression on her face didn't either.

"How long has she been missing? Who was she last with? What was she wearing when you last saw her?" The woman behind the glass wall wearing the second-skin shirt rapidly asked questions like tennis balls catapulting from a machine. This rapid fire made Ma even more befuddled than when she'd first returned home from work to find Noemi not there.

"I don't know," Ma shook her head and cried, adding more tears to the dried up ones on her face. "I don't know the answers to any of these questions."

Ma stared at Jasmin, as if to find answers, but she didn't know either. She didn't know where Noemi was. She didn't even know what she was wearing when they walked to school that morning. Jasmin thought about the answers to these questions, reaching as far back as her mind would let her. She tried to conjure an image in her mind but nothing materialized. Not one answer to any of those questions came to mind. It was like she was taking a test. As much as she studied, as much as she prepared, as much as she actually knew the work, put a test in front of her and all the answers disappeared. She knew, but none of the answers came. Jasmin's chest began to tighten. Slowly, she breathed and quietly calmed herself. *One. Two. One. Two.* She counted.

With no answers, Jasmin put her challenges aside and tried to console Ma who will most likely flood the building with her new tears. She tried to drape her arm around her mother's shoulder, but Ma shoved her handbag towards her to cradle instead.

"I'll buzz you in!" the woman urged. Nothing else mattered at this point. Not the thing she was staring at before they walked in, not the shirt Jasmin imagined was squeezing her to death, not nothing. She didn't ask for identification, nothing. She let Ma and

Jasmin in and they disappeared behind that part of the wall that wasn't plastic.

School-Night Sausage Slam

It doesn't matter how hungry you are, still ask permission. Don't. I repeat: Do Not leave the pot unattended.

Ingredients

3 cups any kind of pasta (already cooked)

1 pound or so of sausage

1 cup of sliced mushrooms

a chopped up medium onion and some celery if you have it

2 cloves garlic, chopped up fine

¼ teaspoon salt

some pepper and paprika

1 ½ cubs broth and ¼ cup all-purpose flour

1 cup sour cream or yogurt (plain)

some chopped parsley or tarragon to sprinkle on top

Cook the meat and vegetables over medium until the meat isn't pink, about 5 minutes. Stir in the spices and flour and then the broth. Bring to a boil but turn down the heat and stir for a couple of minutes until thickened. Then, take it off the heat and stir in the sour cream or plain yogurt. Serve it over the pasta. Yum!

Please clean up afterwards. No one likes a dirty kitchen.

Then

"Noemi!" From the kitchen, Ma screamed in her not-playing-around-voice, "Jasmin? Come down here! NOW!"

Of course, Jasmin heard her since her unlocked door always spread itself wide open like smearing peanut butter across a slice of bread. No matter what, Noemi kept her door closed and locked, even though Ma claimed there'd be no closed or locked doors in her house. *Closed doors are for people who pay rent and who are pooping,* Ma often said. Neither Jasmin nor Noemi paid rent, but still Noemi not only closed her door, she sometimes locked it too. Ma'd always try to open Noemi's locked door which bred their constant fights. Jasmin stayed in her room and listened to their screaming. Never would she interfere from fear of both her mother and her sister. She couldn't choose sides. Noemi stood on her need for privacy and Ma stood behind her house and her rules. Ma's win only lasted until Noemi locked her door again.

"Yeah, Ma," Jasmin yelled back.

"Don't *yeah Ma* me!" she shouted.

"Yes, Ma!" Jasmin quickly corrected.

"Where's your sister?" she asked. "I called the both of you!"

Who cares? was what Jasmin wanted to say but instead answered, "in her room."

"Why is the kitchen like this?" she shouted. "I specifically asked that the kitchen not be left like this. You girls are old enough to know better. You do not have a maid. I AM NOT YOUR SLAVE!" She rubbed her forehead and squinted like her eyes burned. "I don't understand why you can't just do what I say. Don't I do what I say?" Ma stared at Jasmin as though she expected an answer, but Jasmin knew better than to respond. She knew better than to answer because talking back was never a wise decision. "How many times must I say this? The kitchen must be kept clean. It's where the food is. Food goes where?"

"In our mouths," Jasmin responded flatly.

"And if it's going in your mouths..."

"It must come from a clean kitchen," Jasmin added.

"This is why we don't eat out."

"I know."

"Then if you know, why is the kitchen like this? Is this not where we prepare our food that's going into *our bodies, into our mouths*?" She enunciated precisely "our bodies" and "our mouths."

Jasmin wanted to roll her eyes but resisted because she'd need them to see later. When Ma behaved like this, the girls knew she was tired of something or tired of everything. Seeing the house, the kitchen especially, in a catastrophic state wasn't helping to rid her of whatever she'd endured at work. Pots, pans, and plates filled the sink. Drinking glasses, cups, and forks sat stranded on the countertops as if they'd lost their way. Light brown circles like ringworms formed on the countertops from where, Jasmin was certain, Noemi moved the bottle of honey from one spot to another without wiping first with a wet rag, something she regularly did.

Jasmin had a ringworm once, though she had been unaware. It itched until Ma finally asked why she was scratching so much. Eventually, Jasmin had to submit to her thorough investigation.

Planted right under Jasmin's right butt cheek, Jasmin had to wait until she got to school to Google an image of a ringworm. Ma said she likely got it from sitting on toilets at school. Jasmin doubted that because she always squatted.

Ma's days weren't easy nor her nights. Ma had two jobs. If you asked her, she'd say she had only one. A Home Health Care Aide, most nights she spent at her clients', but in fact, most days she wasn't home either. She went from one house to the other, taking care of old, sick people. If she was lucky, her client would sleep through the night and she'd catch some sleep too, but that was rare.

She never worked the same schedule. Sometimes the client's kids gave her time off, until they realized all of the work involved. Eventually, they'd get tired of cleaning up after their own sick parents. If one of her clients died, she'd find a new one immediately. No shortage of jobs since most people neglected their ailing parents. Most people didn't want to clean up after grown folks, she'd say. She'd tell the girls stories of one sibling pawning off the job to another until eventually, they'd have to hire someone like her to do what they wouldn't. She'd say, *I hope my children don't behave that way after I've worked two jobs to make sure that they have everything that they need.* Noemi would quickly respond with, *Of course not, Ma, you'll live with me forever!* Both girls knew that was fantasy. Ma most likely would end up with Jasmin.

Ma missed a lot of the girls' activities at school too because of her hectic schedule. She didn't pass up a job. Even if she wasn't scheduled to work, if someone called her, she'd work, and they wouldn't see her for days and sometimes nights. If she did attend their school activities, she didn't stay long or she fell asleep during a performance. Neither rude nor lazy, she was simply tired. Jasmin understood. They needed food to eat. Ma's work provided that.

They needed a place to live. Ma's work provided that. They needed clothes to wear. Ma's work provided that.

Their father, the little that Jasmin knew of him, did his best until he didn't, according to Ma. She said he was bound to die young, whatever that meant. Sometimes Jasmin created memories in her head of what she should possibly remember of him: being held in his arms, being rocked, hearing some loved tune hummed. Did she remember him reading to her while mimicking a different voice for every character? Did she remember him gliding down the slide at the playground? Did she remember him picking her up and throwing her into the sky all in one motion, while she giggled? Did she remember him picking her up out of the crib, although Ma told him to *let her cry*? Jasmin could totally imagine Ma's ruthlessness. But in her imaginations, her dreams, her father defied Ma's strict rules. Jasmin didn't miss this though, because she didn't know whom to miss. Only Ma was her parent.

Uncle Dee helped, but no one thought him a real adult, and definitely, not Ma. As Ma's only sibling, he could easily pass as the girls' older brother, just by the way Ma treated him. Nothing that he did indicated he was more mature than the girls at all. In fact, everything he did, in Ma's words, was idiotic. He visited only when he needed something. (Ma's words, again.) And, his visits were infrequent. Normally, he'd tap on the door, so quietly that they'd only hear if they were in the living room. He'd speak the normal pleasantries out of duty. *How you and your sister?* Then he'd look around as if chased by a phantom. *How was school? You still in school, right?* His questions never waited for an answer. His eyes darted around looking for Ma. The girls were accustomed to his routine. Then he'd ask *Where's Grace at? She home?* If so, the girls would disappear into their rooms. Ma and Uncle Dee would argue loudly and, then, he'd leave. If Ma weren't home, he'd sometimes wait impatiently and then leave, but he'd return, renewing the cycle. So, Uncle Dee and Ma, plus the pretend memories of her father filled Jasmin's mind.

Since Uncle Dee never attended school activities when Ma couldn't, sometimes Stephen filled in. Jasmin met Stephen a long time ago, in middle school. She often sat by herself during lunch, not a big deal. She preferred sitting solo rather than having a heap of people at her table, talking, saliva spewing from many directions over her food. This was really for the best - a safety precaution really. One day, however, Stephen sat at her table, uninvited. Except for the smacking of mouths, the har-de-har of laughter, and the occasional scream of one kid chasing another around the cafeteria, they commiserated in silence. They ate together an entire week until one day, between bites of his chicken fingers, Stephen asked, "You know, introverts make up an estimated 25% to 40% of the population?" Jasmin had no clue what he was talking about, but with these words they'd become friends. So, he'd often join her when she had to sit and watch Noemi's performances.

Theatre wasn't one of Noemi's electives but she tried out for everything and usually landed a role that had her on stage in more than one scene. That meant that Jasmin had to stand in for Ma because *as siblings, you're all each other's got*. But she still had to go even when Ma could because they were still all each other had. Eventually, Ma'd say, *you've got that boy, Stephen. He can go with you. I'd be at the next one, for sure.* "For sure" usually turned into "*the next one,*" then, "*the next one.*" Last year, Noemi played the role of Cinderella in the school's musical. She wouldn't let Jasmin hear the end of it. Not only did she have to listen to her sing every song and word of dialogue, but Jasmin had to endure hours of rehearsals. By the time it was over, Jasmin wished Cinderella would leave town. Plus, Jasmin hated musicals. Why sing when you could just speak whatever it is you had to say? Of course, most of her performances were nauseating musicals.

Couldn't Jamin just record it for Ma? She couldn't. Ma didn't like electronics, those "evil things" that rotted the brain. She didn't have a smartphone because she insisted they were "spy tools." Who would want to peek into their boring lives? As reality T.V., they'd be canceled by the second episode; no, by the first. Nothing interesting there. Of necessity, they had a phone at home; however, this rang more than Ma's flip phone. When her job switched from pagers, she gave in, otherwise, she'd never walk around with one. Ma said smartphones were the "dumbest things ever invented." So, Noemi and Jasmin felt like the only two teenagers in the entire world who didn't own cell phones.

One time, Stephen placed his phone down on the kitchen counter. It was just for a few moments. Not even long enough for a t.v. commercial and Ma screamed at him. "Put that thing away!"

"What thing?" Stephen asked, confused.

"Your phone," Ma made air-quotes. "You know they use those things to record us."

"Yeah, Step-hen," Noemi mocked Stephen.

Stephen, however, obeyed cramming the phone back in his pocket to put Ma at ease again.

Ma still wore her uniform, a flowered top and pants, both pale pink. Though not required to wear a uniform, she insisted that her employers saw she was a professional. Her words. She hadn't had a chance to change into her ratty looking house dress, which should lie quietly dead in a landfill.

Jasmin waited for her to calm down. "Look!" She pointed to the large calendar on the wall. "Today's Friday, Ma!"

"So?"

"Today's Noemi's day to do the kitchen." Each day of the calendar marked chores. Today, the bathroom was cleaned and her name clearly not written on today's date for kitchen duty, Noemi's was.

"Noemi!!!!!!" Ma screamed.

Jasmin and Ma waited for Noemi to come down the stairs so that they could sort this out. Jasmin wanted Ma to witness the words on the calendar. Besides, plenty of times Jasmin did Noemi's share of the chores just so that they wouldn't have to go through an argument. Yet, she received no credit at all, none from Ma, and definitely, none from Noemi.

"Noemi!!!!" Ma screamed again. "Where is she?"

Jasmin shrugged her shoulders. Knowing Noemi, she was probably in her room, behind her closed and locked door, defying Ma.

"Go get her," Ma demanded. "And don't shrug your shoulders."

Jasmin leaped the stairs two by two. Just as she suspected, Noemi's door stayed closed - a broken rule. She knocked lightly, light enough so that Ma wouldn't realize her door was closed, but loud enough so that Noemi could hear.

Silence.

No shouting at her to go away.

Jasmin knocked again, still lightly.

Silence.

No shuffling around as to hide something.

Jasmin slowly turned the doorknob and risked something thrown at her but decided to avoid another Close Door Lecture. Jasmin guardedly peeked inside.

"Noemi," she whispered, "Ma wants you,"

Silence.

Jasmin pushed the door wider to cautiously step in.

"Noemi?"

Noemi hated trespassing, screaming at Jasmin like a stranger. Noemi, on the other hand, obeyed no such structure with Jasmin's room, taking whatever she wanted, whenever she wanted.

"Noemi?" Jasmin stepped in farther.

Nothing.

Jasmin walked around to the side of the bed where she hoped to see Noemi lying flat on her stomach on the floor, but still no Noemi.

"Noemi?" Jasmin whispered into the empty atmosphere but not even the air responded.

Now

"**I**'m detective Shawn Sanchez!" A tall, lanky man introduced himself.

Weird, Jasmin thought because he didn't look like a Sanchez. Maybe Jackson, Brown, Jones, Freeman? With both sides of his head shaven clean, a light sheet of black hair covered the top of his head. Jasmin examined him from head to toe, noticing his scuffed shoes and mismatched socks, one solid and the other polka dotted, neither matching his khaki pants, white buttoned-down shirt and likely clipped-on tie. To Jasmin, he looked no more like a detective than a senior at her high school.

Lacking a protruding donut-fed belly, he seemed somewhat fit under his clothes, muscles straining gently on his sleeves. *Don't all cops know how to tie a tie,* she wondered. *Barry Allen does.* Jasmin suspected he must be a rookie.

Ma shook his hand, but Jasmin continued to cradle Ma's purse.

"This way, please." He led them to a row of cubicles pointing out his.

Jasmin imagined eyes looking up from their cubicles as they walked by, wondering just as Jasmin and her mother wondered. *I'm glad it's night time*, Jasmin mused. *Less eyes. Nothing like what's on The Flash.*

The cubicle was sparsely decorated with a slightly tilted wall calendar lodged against the soft partition of the cubicle; the desk held a big black phone with its own mini screen. No pictures of

Sanchez on a Harley or with a cat. Impersonal, this cubicle could be anyone's. Grabbing a spare chair from the cubicle across from his, Sancez dragged it across the carpet. They all sat.

It was quiet for a police station, on a Friday night. Jasmin pictured a place with more movement, more action; uniformed officers carting in prostitutes and drug dealers, taking them to the cells. In her mind, boards pinned with pictures and red yarn led from one clue to the other. A lone convict escaping from the grips of an officer and racing through the police station with no obvious exit. But, it was nothing like that.

"Mrs. Hobson?" His voice was soft, sympathetic.

"It's Miss," Jasmin corrected him.

"I'm sorry," he apologized, but looked at Jasmin instead of Ma, the obvious adult. "Miss Hobson, what's your daughter's name?"

"Noemi Hobson," Jasmin answered because Ma was inconsolable.

"Naomi?" he asked and spelled out what he thought it was. "N, a, o, m, i?"

"No," Jasmin said, "it's N, o, e, not N, a, o, it's pronounced Know-e-me."

Ma was crying so much that Sanchez reached into his desks and pulled out napkins, not tissues from a box but brown folded paper ones from a fast food place. In fact, they looked like the same ones that Wendy's had, brown and soft enough for nuggets but too hard for your face. He gave them to her. Like a foghorn, she blew her nose and wiped her tears in two quick motions. He reached into the drawer again for a yellow notepad and began to write. *Why hadn't he had this before he started asking questions? Definitely a rookie mistake,* Jasmin thought.

"Her last name is also Hobson?" he asked.

What else would it be? Jasmin wanted to respond, but instead she said "Yes." She spelled that out for him to scribble on his yellow pad.

We all have the same last name. Why wouldn't we? As far as I knew, Ma was married until she wasn't. With a dead husband, my father, I imagine that Ma wouldn't bother to change her name. Weird question, Jasmin thought.

"I assume she..."

"Noemi," Jasmin interjected. Unlike Ma, Jasmin didn't believe that Noemi was missing, though she did believe she was caught up somewhere doing something she was not supposed to be doing, unable to get home before Ma. Jasmin thought she was in her room like always, ignoring her, doing her own thing. But, no. So, Jasmin was at the police station with Ma doing what she thought was the right thing for her child who she thought was missing. So, spell her name correctly, pronounce her name correctly, and, certainly, do not refer to Noemi as *she*. Detective Olivia Benson also said *call them by name.* Jasmin was glad she watched her shows because clearly Ma didn't know how this worked.

"I'm sorry," Detective Shawn apologized. Sanchez? He seemed entirely too young for Jasmin to call him by his last name. That was for old people. "I assume Noemi goes to school?"

"Yes," Jasmin said. "We go to the same school. She's a year ahead of me but still in the same school."

"Ok," he scribbled on his yellow pad.

Jasmin couldn't imagine his plan because he still hadn't asked what she thought were important questions. When did you see her last? What was she wearing? What does she look like?

"Yes, she's in school," Ma crawled out of her crying coma. "Why wouldn't she be in school? She's a child."

"I need to ask," Shawn put the pencil in his mouth, chewing on it like he was thinking about something. "Some kids take class online, and-"

"Noemi is not *some kids!*" Ma completely cut him off. Her words were scathingly sharp and her tears had long crept back into the ducts they came from. "She is an honor roll student who attends school regularly. She is missing! If she was at school, we would not be here, in front of you, answering these ridiculous questions!"

Jasmin wanted to tell Ma that this was what they did. This was what was needed to find Noemi, who Jasmin couldn't believe was missing. But she didn't say anything. She also wanted to tell Ma that Noemi hadn't been on the honor roll for some time now, but kept this information to herself. This certainly wasn't the time to remind Ma that she hadn't had the time to look at their report cards the way she used to. Things had been different once the girls started high school.

Ever since Jasmin could remember, she and Noemi had to place their report cards on the kitchen counter as soon as they were printed. Ma'd go over them with a fine tooth comb, asking questions like why'd you get an 89 in this class? Couldn't you try harder? Then, they'd head off to *Krispy Kreme* where they earned a donut for each of their A's. Noemi always collected more donuts than Jasmin, always. Later, Ma seemed busier than when the girls were in elementary school, so she stopped looking at report cards altogether and the girls stopped earning donuts.

Jasmin knew that Ma wasn't looking at the report cards even though the girls still placed them on the kitchen counter like they knew they were supposed to. Plain as day, Noemi's C's danced from the paper and Ma didn't scream at her or nothing. She couldn't have known. If she did, Noemi'd be dead, and they wouldn't be sitting at the police station filing this missing person's report. *I bet she's home already,* Jasmin thought.

"Sorry, Miss Hobson," Detective Shawn's voice dragged Jasmin out of her thoughts. "I'm going to have to ask some questions that are seemingly uncomfortable."

This is uncomfortable. Mister, we are in a police station looking for my sister. How much more uncomfortable is it going to get?

Ma tapped her foot on the rug, "Go, on, I just need to find my daughter."

"Each question I'm about to ask you is a routine question." Detective Shawn looked at Ma reluctantly and cracked his knuckles one by one, each protesting loudly. "Go on," Ma demanded. "I just need to find my daughter."

<u>Sanchez's Simple Donuts</u>

Still ask permission. Share if the first batch isn't so good. 😐

Ingredients

2 cups baking mix like Giffy or Bisquick

⅓ cup milk

1 egg

2 tablespoons sugar

some cinnamon

1) Preheat oven to 400°

2) Mix together the baking mix, milk, egg, sugar, and cinnamon. Use a whisk or wooden spoon hard for about 20 - 30 spins around the bowl.

3) Put flour on the cutting board, a clean counter, or tray. Spread it out lightly.

4) Dump the dough onto this floured surface, mooshing it together 5 -10 times. Then, take a rolling pin and roll the ball flat, maybe about ½" and back.

5) Take a clean drinking class and a clean shot glass. Cut out a circle with the drinking glass and then cut its middle out with the shot glass for a donut shape. Don't throw the insides out! Either roll them back into the flat dough or bake them as donut holes.

6) Bake for about 7 - 9 minutes until light brown

7) After they cool, you can frost them with Nutella!

Then

"You believe she's letting us go to the movies?" Jasmin asked Noemi excitedly. As usual, she paid Jasmin no mind. Noemi sat at the kitchen table and stared at her opened textbook. She hadn't turned the page since Jasmin walked in, and she'd been there long enough for her to turn the page at least once.

Jasmin thought back to the last time Ma allowed them to go to the movies without her. It didn't turn out well. Ma was so mad because they'd gotten home so late that it seemed as though steam escaped from her head when they walked into the house. They. No. *Noemi decided* they'd watch a double feature, forcing them to return home much later than the time that Ma'd stated. *Be where you're supposed to be when you're supposed to be there*, were the words that reverberated in Jasmin's mind and *Outside is dangerous. I knew I shouldn't have let you go. Next time... No. There won't be a next time.* Since then, which seemed like a really long time, the girls hadn't been trusted to be on an outing on their own.

Dishes overflowed in the sink like they didn't live in cupboards. Jasmin washed them, wiped the counter tops, careful to leave the kitchen sparkling clean, "for cooking and eating," just the way Ma liked. Jasmin didn't like washing dishes and cleaning up after Noemi, but she really wanted to go to the movies. So, she cleaned and wiped, then cleaned and wiped some more. It was a rare occasion when their mother allowed them to go out, but she'd been so overwhelmed at work lately that she had loosened her reins on the girls. *As long as the chores are done*, Ma said. *And make sure you stay to-ge-ther*. This, the girls knew, was the most important part. *Stick together, no matter what.*

Ma was extremely protective. She often said, *I have two beautiful flowers that I have to take care of or they'll die. Don't walk next to vans with no windows or don't walk next to vans period. If you see a van coming, speed up. Don't talk to strangers. Pay attention to your surroundings. Don't leave your food unattended and go back to it. Leave it be.* The girls had a number of things that they had to remember. Being a single parent didn't help the girls' case for freedom either. Ma's goal was to spend as much time with the girls as possible, but it didn't happen. She didn't want to miss out on raising the girls, but it was happening. Ma was spending less time at home and less time with the girls.

Besides regulating the Maxi pads, Ma was convinced that keeping the girls home was the best birth control. But as far as Jasmin knew, she nor Noemi had no interest in sex. Jasmin certainly wasn't interested in anything that would prevent her from being the top forensic scientist in the country. Dick Wolf would ask her to consult on one of his shows eventually. Jasmin had real plans, plans she wouldn't let sex ruin. Sex, according to Ma, would ruin their entire life. When the girls asked to go out, Ma's response was always, *You wanna get pregnant?!*. Usually Jasmin countered, *Ma, how we gonna get pregnant at the mall? We just gonna hang out.* Ma'd shoot back with, *that's how it starts. I know lots of babies that were conceived from "just hanging out."* At that point, the girls would concede, leaving Ma to her peculiar opinions. Eventually, the girls stopped asking. When other kids would socialize, they were left out.

This sanctioned trip to the movies was a welcomed surprise because according to Ma's theory, people got pregnant there too. Either way, the girls were glad for the permission to leave the house and to go anywhere other than school.

"I'm almost finished with the dishes," Jasmin said as she loaded the dishwasher for an extra rinse. "...then we can leave. You look up the movie? You hear me?" Jasmin yelled.

No answer.

"Noemi!" She yelled again.

No answer.

Noemi often disappeared like a ninja or spider. One minute there, and the next, gone. She moved around with cat-like reflexes, quiet as a mouse, sleek as a snake. Or was it sly as a fox?

Jasmin dried her hands on the towel, folded it to hang on the oven's handle. She ran up the stairs taking them two by two. If they didn't leave, they'd relinquish the opportunity. Ma didn't want them out when it was dark. Although Ma wasn't around, Jasmin always felt like she was, like she had all-seeing eyes that followed them. The last thing she wanted to do was disobey Ma. So, although Ma was allowing the girls to go to the movies, they both knew her rigid rules. At the pace Noemi was moving, the girls were running out of time.

At the top of the stairs, Jasmin could hear clickety-clacking at the computer. A little desk at the top of the stairs housed only the computer. Ma said it didn't need to be any bigger because it would collect junk. The girls were actually very fortunate to even have a computer. It wasn't sleek like the ones at school that looked like flat televisions. A huge piece stuck out of the back of it like an unwanted pimple. Why couldn't Ma get them the sleek, flat screen? The girls had no idea, but they worked with what they had because left to Ma, they'd be no form of technology nowhere near the house. If it wasn't necessary for homework, they definitely wouldn't have one. Without the computer, they'd have to go to the library and that meant leaving the house. Earning good grades trumped Ma's technology insanity any day. However, having the computer often came with Ma's comment of, *when I was in school, we only used paper and I came out fine*. Did she? That was arguable according to the girls.

Jasmin hovered over Noemi hoping she'd chosen the right movie. She didn't want to watch another of her mushy, lovey-dovey movies and most definitely not a musical. Unfortunately, Noemi always got to choose, forcing everyone to bend to her will. Jasmin didn't want to watch a sad movie; she wanted action, some shoot 'em up kind of movie. She reached for the computer screen to turn it, just a bit, towards her.

"I got it!" Noemi pushed Jasmin's hand back as though she'd reached into her plate for her food. She didn't like that either.

Jasmin asked suspiciously, "Well, what are we going to see?"

"Nothing!" She snapped.

"Nothing?" What had she been doing all this time? Definitely not dishes! Jasmin's jaws tightened, but she stayed quiet a few beats. "Look," Jasmin complained. "Ma don't normally let us go."

"I know," Noemi agreed.

"So, let's go, cause you know she don't want us out late neither."

"I know that too."

"Well, move," Jasmin lightly shoved the chair.

"I'm coming," Noemi moved from the chair, "you can pick the movie though,"

"What? You never let me do that!" Jasmin said, surprised.

"I don't care. Pick whatever you want."

Jasmin didn't argue. She just sat down and clicked on Chrome's history just to realize it was gone, no past websites. Noemi had wiped it completely clean.

"Why'd you do that?" Jasmin complained.

"What?" Noemi asked innocently.

"That," Jasmin pointed at the screen, "didn't you have the movies on the screen?"

"So?"

"So?" Jasmin repeated frustratingly.

"You're a parrot now?"

Continuing would've probably started an argument that would've morphed into a fight, a fight that Jasmin was not going to win. Noemi towered over Jasmin on her long, shapely legs. Meanwhile, Jasmin could easily be mistaken for a black penguin. Noemi's body revealed the shape of a fully developed teenager, while Jasmin couldn't fill a bra unless she tied it around her chest. Noemi's waist was tiny while Jasmin's looked like it could be the pouch of a Caprisun. Noemi's long, black, thick hair met Jasmin's thin ponytail. Jasmin felt sensitive to those contrasts.

Other times Jasmin had caught her deleting emails that said *your son or daughter has a D or F in one or more of their classes.* Each time, she'd claim it was a mistake, but they both knew better. Noemi was lucky that Ma never saw them or she'd be dead as she would have had she been on social media. According to Ma, those accounts could get you pregnant too. So, no Instagram, nor Snapchat. Definitely not Facebook because that was for old people.

"The next one starts in thirty five minutes," Jasmin yelled, hoping her voice traveled down the hallway, "so we gotta go now!"

They weren't far from the mall, walking distance. As long as Noemi didn't stop at any of the stores, they would arrive on time. Jasmin hated to miss the previews.

"Go downstairs," Noemi responded, "I'll be there in a minute."

"I'm not playing, Nome!" Jasmin called her by her nickname. A name Ma said Jasmin developed when she couldn't quite pronounce her name correctly as a baby. She'd stop at *Nome. Nome. Nome.*

A rustling sound came from Noemi's room like she was opening a heavily wrapped Christmas gift, but it was nowhere near Christmas. Jasmin left her and hurried downstairs. The less she saw, the less she'd have to answer. They had to go and go soon, one minute turned into twenty, and then, twenty one. Now, they'd miss the previews. Jasmin chewed on the inside of her jaws to keep from yelling.

"Nome!" She screamed and hoped her voice made it up the stairs. "Let's go! The movie's about to start, and you know I hate missing the previews."

Noemi sauntered down as though they had all the time in the world, like the sun would wait for them, like the previews weren't going to start until their arrival. Her face was coated with fake-up, make-up Jasmin knew Ma didn't buy, make-up that made her look like someone's Ma herself. Make-up that she knew she wasn't allowed to wear. Jasmin's eyes roamed from Noemi's garish face to the sleeveless denim jacket that barely covered her flimsy sports bra and then to her exposed belly that revealed a shiny metal ring that protruded from her nave. *Ma's going to kill you*, Jasmin thought. Noemi's ripped shorts hung loosely. She looked like one of those girls Ma warned them to stay away from, a girl who looked like she did the kind of things that would keep Jasmin from becoming the top forensic scientist in the world.

What the heck Noemi? Jasmin wanted to say, but instead said, "Let's go!" pretending not to notice.

In spite of Noemi's rebellious spirit, Jasmin couldn't help but think about how it'd be living this carefree life Noemi led. Jasmin secretly admired Noemi's ability to break away from Ma's rules, without Ma knowing. Was she stifling herself by worrying? *Relax.* Jasmin told herself. *If I could do it, I would, but at least one of us should follow the rules, right?*

Capri Sun Popsicles

Take the straw that comes with the pouch and poke a hole in the bottom, holding upside down so it doesn't spill.

Put a popsicle stick in the hole and freeze till solid.

cut open and now you have a popsicle!

Now

The police station began to hum with workers, some walking-around busy, some with uniforms, some without. Still Jasmin couldn't tell who was a forensic scientist.

It felt like hours had passed as they, mostly Jasmin, answered unrelenting questions but actually only minutes had passed. It seemed like the clock on the wall was broken staring at them like it didn't have a job. It was like that clock on the board when students were testing. If they knew the answers, the clock didn't move: however, if the answers evaded them, it was as though the clock was running a race it must win. Did they ask many questions for every teenage girl who couldn't be found? Olivia Benson did, but that was just a T.V. show.

"Are you certain that she didn't run away?" he asked without blinking, continuing to write on his yellow pad.

Fidgeting at the table as though she was trying to hold her tongue, Ma could chew him and spit him out with only a few words, but she needed his help. Immediately, she stopped the tears. Her eyes were squarely focused on the young man. He was about to die by the hands of Ma but he didn't even know it. It was as if her eyes sucked up all her tears, as the sun could drain a pond. Bit by bit the ponds dried as the sun did its damage. This was Ma. She changed from an inconsolable mother to one who had had her cookie stolen. Jasmin had seen this before, a different Ma. Once while shopping, the cashier was rude and Ma morphed into another person. Those on the receiving end always ended up regretting their actions.

"Why would you say that?" Ma's voice was edgy. "Why would you say that?" she repeated.

Ma's eyes darted to the detective's head. If she had laser beams, he'd be lying on his desk, a smoking head, dead.

"Look," she said firmly, "this is the tenth time you've asked me this doltish question."

Jasmin wanted to disappear into a dark hole, because Ma was seething now. She was about to tear this guy apart but they needed his help, even if he looked like he was Jasmin's age. With this behavior, there was no way they would send a search party for Noemi, no way. Her helpless face turned to one of outright anger. Very few times Ma morphed into this person, but when she did, woe to the person on the receiving end.

One time they went to Six Flags over Georgia, a big vacation since Ma took time off work. Uncle Dee went along probably only for a free vacation for him. On that road trip, Dee slept the whole time, but that's also the trip the girls saw Ma her angriest. In the middle of the night, the time when most vampires found their prey, they pulled into the hotel parking lot. Dim street lamps revealed a few people hanging out, never a good thing. Ma parked, reluctantly. After she got the keys, she drove around to their rooms, one for Uncle Dee because no one would share a room with his loud snoring self. Jasmin knew it was a bad hotel. It reminded her of one of those hotels on CSI, one where they'd find a dead body every weekend. In spite of the obvious negative signs: people on the stairs smoking, clothes hanging on the railings, large stuffed plastic bags outside doors, they entered their rooms. Noemi screwed up her nose immediately. Jasmin didn't say anything. The sheets hadn't looked washed. On the floor lay the remote and garbage peeked from the waste bin.

"It's been a long trip," Ma looked around and sighed. "Let's just take a shower and get ready for Six Flags in the morning." She whispered woohoo so weakly that there was no way she even believed herself.

Noemi and Jasmin sat on each of the two beds staring at each other in hopes they didn't have to stay. From the little they saw of hotels from T.V., they understood that this wasn't right. Ma undressed and headed to the bathroom. Within seconds, she exited to hurriedly redress.

"We're leaving!" she declared and started paging through a big yellow book that sat on the small round corner table.

Although they planned to stay for a week, Jasmin and Noemi hadn't unpacked yet. To avoid FAMILY FOUND DEAD IN SEEDY HOTEL! They would sleep in their clothes as they did during a terrible hurricane. That night, Ma called another hotel for them to stay in. They fetched uncle Dee and headed to the front desk.

They all tramped inside with Ma rather than stay in the van.

"Problem?" the lady behind the desk asked, sarcastically.

"Well that's an understatement," Ma countered.

"And?"

"I need my money back."

"Why, what's going on?" she asked.

"Your rooms are unsafe, unclean, and we're not staying in them. Therefore, I need my money back!"

"I can't give you a refund," she said flatly. "You've already been in the room."

"It's been less than an hour," Ma rubbed her temple. She did that when she was tired and frustrated. "I need my money back."

"That's not something I can do," she persisted.

"Look," Ma shouted. Then she looked at the girls and Uncle Dee and said, "Dee take the girls to the van." The girls knew what was coming and quickly followed Uncle Dee to the van. They peered through the window only to see Ma's hands flailing in the air like a mad woman's. While they didn't know her words, they knew Ma. Needless to say, she walked out that nasty office counting her money, the last time Jasmin had heard her tell someone "Look."

"Look!" Ma repeated to the detective.

The detective must've seen the imaginary cartoon smoke spewing from her ears too because he quickly changed his tone and met her eyes when he spoke.

"Actually, Ms..." he stumbled over his words as they piled onto each other. "Ms. Hobson, in most cases -"

"This is not MOST cases! My daughter has a great home, her own room, everything she wants and needs."

Jasmin slightly shook her head no but uttered nothing to disagree.

"I understand what you are saying, but -"

Ma butted in. "You understand nothing! She did not run away. Not this family. That's not how it works. I've given her nothing to run from."

Jasmin could have reminded Ma how she kept them as protected as Drake's jewelry but again, not the time to kick her when she's wrong. *Is that the saying*?

The detective said, "Ms. Hobson, if you'd just..."

"Not ALL black girls run away, you know. Some actually go..." She glanced at her folded hands as tears began to seep.

Shawn gently asked for a recent picture of Noemi and Jasmin thought of Noemi's picture on a light pole, like a lost dog. Ma found her most recent picture taken just a few months ago in school. Ma took it right out of her wallet and Jasmin wondered if Ma could find hers as quickly.

Then

Jasmin tried her best to ignore Noemi's attire but failed. It was just a movie for crying out loud. Jasmin wondered why she had to dress like she was one of Cardi B's back up dancers. Her shorts were torn to the point where her pocket was seeping through the hole. Could it even store anything? Jasmin loved pockets because they allowed her to store anything in them, a pen, keys, those powdery red and white mints. Not chocolate though because that'd melt for sure. But, there was no way Noemi's pockets could hold a thing. *What's the sense in even shorts so short?* Jasmin wondered.

Jasmin couldn't help herself, so she said, "Why are you wearing that?"

Noemi's stride continued, one long leg in front of the other as though Jasmin hadn't said anything, as though she would've worn the same thing had Ma been with them. Car after car whizzed by. Some honked their horns, Jasmin hoped, unintentionally, because no matter what, Noemi was still a teenager. Jasmin wanted to tell Ma so badly but not enough to threaten her freedom. Plus, she wasn't a snitch. *Heard that in a movie.*

"Why are you even dressed like that?" Jasmin pressed.

"Why are you worrying about me?"

"Where'd you even get these clothes from?"

Noemi rolled her eyes. Jasmin wished they'd get stuck in her head the way Ma always said one day they would.

"Again, do not worry about me," Noemi brushed imaginary lint off her jeans jacket and continued to walk.

They turned into the plaza to only the sounds of cars passing and their footsteps. The sun had almost set but the movie theater's sign did not light up the night. Cars filled the parking lot which meant it was definitely going to be challenging to get the seats they wanted. Jasmin didn't hate much, but she hated being forced to sit in seats that left her neck stiff. They were in that situation she was trying so hard to avoid.

Frustrated, Jasmin sped up. *Forget Noemi!* She thought.

Noemi lagged behind, continuously adjusting pieces of her clothing at every turn. Pulled her shorts from her butt. Repeatedly looked down at her shirt and picked imaginary lint off of it.

Why wear what caused so many problems? Jasmin wondered. It wasn't worth it. Her t-shirt and jeans were just fine, plus, Noemi was definitely going to freeze in the cold theater.

Jasmin lined up for the tickets. It wasn't as long as she'd anticipated but, maybe because people were already inside or maybe because the theater was lodged between Dillard's and JC Penney's. Jasmin tried to be optimistic about seats.

"Jaz!" Noemi rushed up to Jasmin just before she got to the counter. She draped her long arm around Jasmin's neck as if they were the best of sisters. There were times when Jasmin felt as though Noemi hated her very existence, like she was in the way or something. With her arm draped around her, this felt good, but Jasmin knew what was coming. She knew Noemi was about to ask a favor. She thought for a moment. She really didn't want to see a musical, but what could she do? Noemi was usually very convincing. She braced herself.

"What?!" Jasmin asked.

"Just buy one ticket!"

"You're watching a different movie?" Was she meeting someone else, so that's why Jasmin chose the movie? Interesting.

"No, but," she bit her nail.

"No, but, what, Noemi?" Jasmin was not in the mood for whatever she was about to say. At least half the previews were over, which Jasmin hated.

"Well," she paused.

"Well?" Jasmin mocked.

With her arm tightly wrapped around Jasmin's neck, Noemi said, "Gonna watch another movie."

"I thought we decided. You chose the last time and now it's my turn. Plus, I hate musicals," Jasmin fumed.

They advanced in the line. Jasmin was certain that people were staring at them like those who held up the line because they were unsure of what snacks they wanted or which movie they wanted to see, without consideration of others waiting behind them. Jasmin didn't want to be those people but Noemi made them *those people*.

"Fine!" Jasmin surrendered. "What are we watching?"

Resigning herself to a musical, she twisted Jasmin's body around so that they faced each other. Staring into Jasmin's eyes as though she were about to reveal the secret codes to a safe filled with money, Noemi said, "You, trust me right?"

"No!" Jasmin said, emphatically. She didn't. Jasmin always ended up on the bad end of Noemi's plans. But Noemi made sure she got credit for the good. She released one of Jasmin's shoulders placing her hand on her chest as though clutching imaginary pearls in pretend shock.

"What movie are you watching?" Jasmin asked suspiciously, "and with who?"

"Nothing you wanna see," she paused, "and no one you know."

Jasmin fumed. Noemi knew that Jasmin didn't like being alone, plus they were to always stick together. That's what Ma said.

"I'll just watch whatever you want," Jasmin surrendered. "I guess with whoever, too."

"I'm good, Jaz."

"Naw, Ma won't like this."

"She wouldn't but how's she going to know?" she asked. "You're going to tell her?"

"I might," Jasmin threatened.

"Right," Noemi answered.

Jasmin always felt like Ma had some sort of sixth sense about them and everything they did. Jasmin felt it was just easier to obey than to deal with the punishment later. Plus, if Ma found out, they were never going to movies ever again. Jasmin was certain that this was going to be one of those times, one of those times where Ma knew before they even got home that they'd disobeyed her.

"Which movie?" The clerk interrupted Jasmin's thoughts. Jasmin told the clerk the name of the movie and waited for Noemi to say the name of her movie, but Noemi said nothing.

Jasmin stared at Noemi and waited again for her to say the name of a musical but, instead she whispered, "I'm not going in."

"Why not?" Jasmin asked. It still hadn't registered.

"Cause I'm not."

"Where are you going?"

"None-ya," she retorted, "but I'll be back before your movie is out. Promise."

Jasmin hadn't noticed the car parked at the curb waiting. It had loud music blaring from it, bass like a loud heart beating and screaming like a rude siren. Noemi walked towards it, opened the passenger door and disappeared behind the loud noise. She knew they weren't supposed to get into cars with strangers. Like a detective, not a forensic scientist, Jasmin peered at the license plate but all she got was...

Nothing.

Now

The detective returned with Noemi's picture and gave it back to Ma. Jasmin wondered if he'd made a copy to place on the board of *Missing Girls* like on T.V. Was Noemi's picture now pushed pinned to a board, yards of yarn leading from hers to another girl's and then to another?

"That's it?" Ma asked before the young detective with his possibly, no, definitely clip on tie sat down.

"No, Mrs.-"

"It's Mizz," Ma emphasized.

"Sorry," the young detective said and fumbled with a manila folder he had. It was thick, as if this case had been worked on for a long time.

How could that be when we've just given him this information on Noemi? Jasmin wondered

"Mizz Hobson," he said Mizz like bees buzzing at the end of the syllable. He didn't plan or didn't want to make the mistake of calling her *Mrs.* "We are going to do everything that we can to... uhm... find your missing daughter."

"Thank you!" Ma said and she began to sob again. Jasmin tried to think of a time that she'd ever seen Ma this distraught. Nothing. Nothing came to mind as she sat inconsolable.

The detective took his seat, put the manila folder on the desk and opened it. Jasmin realized that its thickness came solely from the yellow notepad on which he'd been taking notes. It wasn't thick from information that could possibly locate Noemi, who, again, Jasmin did not think was *missing*. She just knew Noemi was going to be home by the time they got back. She was going to be in her room acting as though she'd been there this entire time, but just didn't hear them calling her. *She's going to be home when we return; I just know it.*

"Can you think of anything?" the detective asked before words could leave Ma's mouth. "Anything at all that can help us in locating your daughter?" he continued as he got out his pen to write on his yellow pad.

Jasmin knew this question. They asked this question a lot on *Law & Order SVU*. They usually followed it up with, "even the things that you may think are not important, usually are."

Ma shook her head, oblivious, and the detective looked at Jasmin and said, "even if you think it's insignificant or not important, it usually is."

Jasmin wanted to say that she knew what *insignificant* meant, but she didn't. She wanted to say that she'd scored a 1500 on her PSAT, but she didn't. She wanted to ask him what he'd scored because she suspected he'd just done his, as young as he looked, but she didn't.

But, this made it official. Asking these types of questions made Noemi's missing status official. Uttering these words solidified this missing-person's case. Noemi was going to get it for sure when she turned up. Ma was making a fuss about nothing. Went all the way down to the police station to make a report about a missing girl who wasn't even really missing. *Ma's gonna be pissed when we get home and Noemi is there,* Jasmin thought.

"What about you?" The detective looked at Jasmin. "Can you think of anything that your mother hasn't already told me? When was the last time you saw her?" The detective looked at Jasmin dubiously. She and Noemi weren't like regular sisters. They didn't braid each other's hair. Matter of fact, if Jasmin even touched Noemi's hair, she'd most likely lose a few of her fingers. They didn't raid each other's closets like Jasmin was sure other sisters did. Plus, nothing Noemi had fit her. Their time together was mandatory. The rule was that they were always supposed to be together, no matter what. While at home, though, Jasmin kept to her space and Noemi's hers.

"Noemi?" Jasmin asked like they hadn't just driven all the way to the police station to report her missing sister. It's not like she had any other sisters or even siblings. *Stupid question, Jasmin.* She thought and answered quickly in hopes that no one else realized that it was stupid. "In school."

"In school?" Ma said, stupefied. "You mean you didn't walk home together?"

"I mean," Jasmin paused because she wanted to tell Ma that Noemi hadn't walked home with them in a long time. It was mostly her and Stephen. She wanted to tell Ma that she barely saw Noemi in school, not because she didn't go but because Noemi's classes were mostly in different buildings from hers. Matter of fact, Jasmin didn't even know where Noemi's classes were. They didn't have the same lunch either so it was not likely that she'd run into her, ever. She wanted to tell her that Noemi didn't do all the things that she thought she did, but instead Jasmin said, "I mean, yeah, we walked home together." She said this and relaxed a little as though this one piece of information ensured they'd find Noemi now.

"So, it wasn't in school?" Detective Sanchez (who didn't look like a Sanchez) searched Jasmin's face.

"Naw, it wasn't school," Jasmin repeated. "We did walk home together, though. She was home with me, until, I guess, she wasn't."

"You guess?" Ma questioned. She was clearly unsure of what had been happening when she was not home. The hours and hours that she missed with the girls were catching up to her and it was beginning to show on her face. Or maybe something else showed on her face. Worry about Noemi?

"I mean," Jasmin paused, choosing her words carefully. "We walked home together."

According to Ma, they were supposed to always be together, but even if they tried to obey her, it was just not possible. Noemi always was a grade ahead. By eighth grade, Noemi was already at the Ninth Grade Center. When Jasmin attended the Ninth Grade Center, Noemi was on the main campus. By the time Jasmin made it to the main campus, Noemi was too popular for her to even notice Jasmin. The few times that they did walk home together, they still weren't really *together*. Noemi was with her friends and Jasmin with hers.

"Okay, so you walked home together. What did you do at home?" Detective Sanchez asked.

Ma looked at Jasmin suspiciously.

"Nothing," Jasmin answered.

"Did someone come by to pick her up?" Detective Sanchez continued.

"No!" Ma pleaded, "Noemi wouldn't have anyone at the house."

Again, Jasmin wanted to correct Ma, tell her that *people* came by the house all the time. But, Jasmin kept her lips sealed so that she didn't contradict Ma's truth. Instead, she shook her head in agreement.

"Can you give me a list of her friends?" Detective Sanchez looked at Jasmin in his ready-to-write position.

"She has no friends," Ma answered for Jasmin. "She has her sister, Jasmin."

Jasmin lowered her eyes because she realized that Ma didn't really know her daughter at all. Jasmin also felt that Detective Sanchez believed that she may know more than she was saying. *But Noemi is home,* Jasmin thought. *She will kill me if I say anything.*

"Is this true?" Detective Sanchez inquired, ignoring Ma. "Jasmin, does Noemi have no friends?"

Isn't this your job to find out if she has friends? Jasmin asked but the words never left her mouth. She instead shook her head, *yes,* agreeing with Ma. If Ma said she had no friends, then the answer was no.

Maybe this was reality after all. Maybe Noemi was indeed missing.

Then

The movie let out over an hour ago. Even allowing for extended credits, but it was a regular movie, with no extended credits, hour and a half long, at the most. No, Jasmin didn't see the previews because she was late.

Jasmin didn't miss Noemi's company or arguing over what movie to see or elbow wrestling over the skinny armrest. And, she certainly didn't miss having to share her popcorn with Noemi because she'd eaten all of hers before the movie even started. Noemi gone meant that Jasmin could enjoy what she wanted for a change: no musical, no mushy movie, no strife.

Noemi left movies all the time: going to the bathroom disappearing mysteriously. But Jasmin? She always got prepared: Popcorn, Twizzlers, peanut M & M's were bought before the show. Jasmin purposely didn't buy drinks to avoid having to get up, missing a vital part.

Jasmin escaped the theater as the heat rushed her face. She wanted to wait in the cool air-conditioning, but she had to find Noemi, and fast because now they had to go home. No black car with loud music appeared, just people lined up for their movie tickets. The strong scent of the popcorn threatened to pull her back, but she stayed focused on finding her sister. Snatches of conversations infused the atmosphere. Words ran into each other; people laughed boisterously. It was much louder than when the girls had first arrived. Clearly a good night for all, but if Noemi didn't show up soon, it wouldn't be as good for Jasmin, not good at all.

At past ten at night the sky was still bright enough to trick someone into believing that it really wasn't that late. *This was what Ma was talking about though,* Jasmin thought, being at home in a decent hour, but they ran out of "decent hour" an hour ago. The parking lot was still filled with cars, people streamed in, some hurried as though they too didn't want to miss the previews while others strolled as though the previews weren't important. More and more people streamed in but no Noemi. Multiple cars drove up and stopped, but Noemi didn't exit any. With each car, loud music or not, Jasmin perked up eagerly like a hungry puppy hearing food falling in its feeding bowl. Noemi said she'd be back before the movie ended. She shouldn't have gone in the first place! Waiting was making it worse, from Jasmin's impatience, but so much more because each minute that passed gave Jasmin time to realize how Noemi could be in danger. An image of a dumpster appeared unwarranted; *that's where most of the victims were found on TV*, she thought. Ma always said, *be where you're supposed to be when you're supposed to be there*. Now, Jasmin panicked fully, hoping that she'd crawl out from one... a car, not a dumpster. *She told me she'd be back before the movie was out*, Jasmin moaned internally.

Because the bench wasn't empty, Jasmin sat on the edge of the pavement. Couples curled up into each other left no space for her. Every car that blared loud music piqued her interest, no matter if the car was black or not. Each time, she anticipated Noemi stepping out hoping she'd show up soon.

Maybe she forgot that I had been waiting for her, Jasmin thought. She wished for Stephen; then she wouldn't have felt so alone. He could tell her statistics about the number of people who like a movie or anything to keep her from worrying. If Stephen were there, people wouldn't stare at her as though contemplating calling the police or giving her a donation. What if Noemi never came back? What if Ma was home already? What could she say that kept them that long? There was not enough explaining in the world to make Ma understand why.

Jasmin noticed students from school, some she knew and others who were popular, so everyone knew them. None of them spoke to her though. They just kept on walking towards their intended destinations. None asked if she needed help or even what she was doing. Jasmin felt slighted by their behavior. *I guess if Noemi doesn't care, why should they,* she thought.

Noemi needed to show up. She knew Jasmin couldn't go home without her. Noemi also knew that there was no way Jasmin would tell Ma that she wasn't at the movie because Jasmin didn't want to lose the few opportunities they were allowed to go to the movies.

One: they weren't supposed to ever split up the way Noemi forced them to. And, two: if Ma found out, that would jeopardize them ever going any place ever again. The little trust that Ma had in them would be gone.

The boom boom of music loudly filled the air but this was not a black car, not like what Noemi left in, but enough to have fooled Jasmin that she put her head back down in order to squeeze her thoughts together. She was certain that she'd die waiting for Noemi. Either way, Ma was going to kill her for sure.

"You ready?" the sound of a familiar voice filled the air.

Jasmin lifted her head from her legs to stare at Noemi who stood as though she hadn't left her there to die. Jasmin was tired of waiting, of wondering, of being angry. But, Jasmin was not too tired to notice that Noemi sported a different outfit now. When did she have time to change? Where did these clothes come from? How did these clothes fit into her little tiny pockets seeping out the edges of her shorts from earlier in the night? This outfit was Ma-appropriate, her khakis just above her knees, no rips, a complete contrast from what she had worn. A plain t-shirt with no holes and a fully sewn denim jacket finalized her outfit.

Jasmin refused to give Noemi the satisfaction of letting her know how angry she was. What good would that do? Noemi'd just make up a story taking no responsibility, acting as though what she had done wasn't wrong, insensitive, or selfish, so, instead, Jasmin quietly seethed preferring to go home.

Jasmin struggled from the ledge where she'd spent what seemed like the majority of the night. As newly named Rip Van Jasmin, her body ached from that position. She ignored Noemi's question. Of course, she'd been ready. She'd been ready since the movie finished, hours ago.

"How was the movie?" Noemi asked, her voice seemingly filled with butterflies and rainbows.

But, Jasmin couldn't remember the name of the movie or tell Noemi what happened, even if she wanted to. But she also wasn't going to tell her that she'd been worried about her. All Jasmin remembered was waiting, and waiting, endlessly waiting for her sister to return after leaving a movie they should've watched together. Jasmin remained silent. Noemi didn't deserve an answer.

Now

Noemi had many people who knew her and knew of her. When Jasmin did see her on campus, which wasn't often, she was often laughing with a group and ignoring Jasmin. She didn't say hi, wave, nothing. So, Jasmin pretended not to see her either.

A member of every activity on campus, Jasmin was certain that Noemi knew everyone and everyone knew her. The theater people alone, the largest group on campus, inhabited every corner of the school. They sat on tables, belting out tunes Jasmin didn't know, as other thespians cheered them on, always an obnoxious scene. Who wanted to hear that while eating? Noemi had been doing this so long so she had to have had a lot of theater friends right?

As an uninvolved sophomore, unlike Noemi, Jasmin kept to a certain spot. She attended classes and lunch but nothing more. The track people, more of Noemi's friends, also appeared everywhere in their tracksuits. No matter how hot it was, they'd wear sneakers, sometimes tiny shorts and oversized-sweaters to simulate extra large mini dresses, always ready for a race it seemed. Noemi didn't dress like that though. Though she had her own style, she somehow fit right in, unlike Jasmin, where her only real friend was Stephen. Noemi knew a lot of people.

This was something Sanchez could discover if he actually investigated... but no. He asked Jasmin questions instead. Ma didn't know anything and Jasmin was certainly not going to reveal Noemi's business for fear of what Noemi may do to her.

"So, she," the detective paused, "Noemi."

Jasmin smiled, satisfied because he finally realized the significance of Noemi's name. Feeling the warmth on her face, Jasmin quickly fixed her face with a stoic expression that it should be in. Smiling in front of a detective who was looking for her presumed missing sister was not the look to have. So, she fixed her face real quick before Ma noticed. Detective Sanchez, though, noticed, but didn't say a word. He didn't call her out but he noticed.

"Yes, Noemi," Jasmin said, hoping that he'd forget. But he wouldn't, not if he was in fact a real detective.

"You say she doesn't have any friends at all?" He asked. "No one she talks to besides you."

"Not really," Jasmin answered.

"*Not really*," the detective echoed. "Let's start there. I'm not saying that you're purposely leaving something out but I want you to think clearly. You say Noemi is an eleventh grader?"

"Yes," Jasmin confirmed. "And, I'm not leaving nothing out."

"Not purposely," he added. "At Spring Park High, right?"

Jasmin thought about that time when Ma acted like she didn't believe her. Both girls walked home from elementary school, kicking stray rocks along the street when some of Noemi's friends joined them. Noemi giggled with them and ignored Jasmin, something she was not supposed to do.

"Noemi," Jasmin pulled at her backpack.

"Stop," Noemi yelled and violently pushed her to the ground.

Noemi and her friends erupted in laughter while Jasmin lay on the ground squeezing her eyes shut to keep the tears from falling. She didn't want to look like a kid in front of Noemi's friends.

"Get up," Noemi walked away yelling. "Let's go."

Blood seeped from Jasmin's leg as she struggled to get up with no help from Noemi. "Nome," Jasmin's small voice squeaked. "I'm bleeding."

"Are you dead?" Noemi yelled back without looking.

Jasmin looked down at her leg to make sure she wasn't dead, then answered, "no."

"Then you're fine." Noemi replied, continuing with her friends. "You better hurry before the boogeyman comes for you."

With blood running down her leg, Jasmin hurried to catch up to Noemi and her friends. Jasmin breathed heavily, finally catching up to Noemi and her friends as they got to the house.

"Really?" Noemi said disgustingly. "Is it really that serious?"

"Yeah," Jasmin cried, freeing the tears now that Noemi's friends were gone.

"Stop it," Noemi said sternly. "Right now."

"It hurts," Jasmin whined.

"What's going on out here?" Ma opened the door before the girls could get inside.

"Nothing, Ma." Noemi said flatly.

"What happened?" Ma rushed to Jasmin's side spotting the semi-dried blood on her leg.

"Noemi pushed me down-" Jasmin began.

"No I didn't," Noemi stared coldly at Jasmin.

"Yeah, she did," Jasmin complained.

"She slipped, Ma." Noemi told Ma. "I tried to help her up but she wouldn't let me."

"She's lying," Jasmin said.

"Okay. Okay." Ma tried to calm down Jasmin. "Let's settle this now. Noemi? Did you push your sister?"

Noemi folded her arms, rolling her eyes, "Of course not, Ma."

"Jasmin?" Ma asked softly. "Is it possible that you tripped and thought while Noemi was helping you up that she may have pushed you?"

Jasmin thought for a moment. Did she imagine Noemi pushing her? If she did, that meant that she'd have to have imagined her friends laughing at her too.

No, Jasmin shook her head.

"The mind is a tricky thing," Ma added.

"It is," Noemi echoed.

I didn't though, Jasmin thought. *I didn't imagine it. I didn't.*

That was the same feeling she got from the detective. *Maybe he thought I was imagining my answers too.*

"Yeah, Spring Park High," Jasmin answered.

"Yes," Ma corrected Jasmin as though proper grammar mattered at a time like this. Jasmin wanted to roll her eyes but stopped as she would most likely need them in the future.

"I went to that school," the detective perked up. "Go Lions!"

"Go Lions," Jasmin intoned unenthusiastically.

"I remember they used to paint all the lions around campus pink for breast cancer month," he mused. "Do they still do that?"

"Yeah," Jasmin said but quickly corrected herself because Ma was still listening. "Yes."

"I remember we'd play all our games in a pink uniform too. Are they still doing that?"

"I don't know," Jasmin answered, unsure because she didn't know what games he meant. To Jasmin, he could be a basketball player with his long legs and lengthy arms, but his muscles under his tight shirt could also mean football too.

"What about my daughter?" Ma interrupted. "What are you going to do about finding her?"

"I'm sorry, Ms. Hobson," the detective apologized. "You said she has a lot of friends."

"I didn't," Jasmin reminded him. She hadn't said anything about Noemi and friends. She gave nothing to Sanchez.

"So, besides you," he looked at Jasmin intensely, ignoring Ma, "is there anyone else you've ever seen her talking to? Anyone at all?"

"Not really."

"Is she a cheerleader?"

"No," Jasmin answered. Why would he even ask that?

"What does she do at school?" he asked. "A club, team, SGA, something?"

"She's in theater and she runs tracks," Ma chimed in.

"And she doesn't have any friends?" the detective eyed Jasmin suspiciously.

"What about..." Ma questioned, but paused.

"Do you know her friends?" The detective directed this question now to Ma because she looked like she was thinking about something that could possibly help.

"That girl?" Ma said. "The one you used to walk home with sometimes? She lives across the street from us. Blonde hair. Slim, like Noemi?"

"That was elementary school, Ma," Jasmin corrected. "She doesn't even go to the same school as us anymore." Jasmin remembered exactly who Ma talked about. That girl hadn't lived in their neighborhood for some time and Jasmin was glad for it.

"Ok," Ma sighed.

"What about her track and theater friends?" the detective asked. "From what I remember, that was a pretty tight group. Everyone stuck together. Not that I was a part of the theater, but you just couldn't tell them apart from each other."

"I'm sure she has friends," Jasmin admitted. "I just don't know who they are."

And she didn't. Jasmin knew that Noemi hung out with a lot of people but to Jasmin, they were nameless. All Jasmin knew was they were just as popular as Noemi. She knew not to speak to Noemi if she happened to run into her with her friends. Jasmin really didn't know much and it was starting to show.

"Ok, tell me again," the detective suggested. "You get home and she's not there. Can you tell me that story again?"

"We've told you this already," Ma fumed.

"It's what they do, Ma," Jasmin informed Ma. On every T.V. show, this is what cops did. The good ones anyway, repeated questions in hopes of catching a lie or helping the witness to reveal pertinent information. Jasmin hoped for the latter because they really had no reason to lie to the police.

"They were already home when I got there and..." Ma paused. "Well, Jasmin was there."

"So, you must've seen something?" The detective directed this question to Jasmin.

She nodded her head *no*.

"Heard something?"

She nodded her head *no*.

Four eyes were on Jasmin now as though she had all the answers, but she didn't. If she did, she'd be with Noemi, wherever she was, hoping to come home too.

"Jasmin, you must've heard or seen something if you were there in the house with Noemi." Ma used her *you better-give-me-some-answers* voice. It was the same as her *these-dishes-better-be-gone-by-the-time-I-get-back* voice, gruff and demanding.

Again, Jasmin nodded her head *no*. She and Noemi were rarely in the same room together. Like the white of the egg and the yolk, they avoided each other as long as possible. Jasmin didn't hear a thing, and if she did, why would she think it was the sound of Noemi leaving. Jasmin didn't dare think of any other possibilities. She didn't want to.

"Ok," the detective breathed heavily. "Then, what was she wearing?"

"I don't know."

"You don't remember what your sister was wearing when you walked home from school?" Ma shouted.

The detective sat up, almost at the edge of his seat.

"We just want you to try your best, Jasmin. This is serious." The detective tried to explain away Ma's anger towards Jasmin. They, the detective and Ma, have now become a *WE*.

"I know it's serious," Jasmin responded. "I really don't know anything, though."

"Where were you when your mother got home?" the detective asked.

This isn't even about me, Jasmin thought but answered, "in my room."

"And where was Noemi?" Ma asked.

"In her room," Jasmin answered. "I guess." She really wanted to say, *I'm not my sister's keeper*, but she didn't dare contradict anything Ma thought. For Ma, she and Noemi were together twenty-four-seven although that was rarely ever the case.

"Your rooms are right next to each other's," Ma said to no one in particular. "How could you not hear anything or see anything? This is why I tell you girls to do your homework together. Keep each other company. Many people don't even have another sibling, someone to be with. You girls should always be together. Like you used to be."

Used to be? Jasmin thought. *Noemi and I had never been together, and I wanted Sanchez to know this. I wanted to remind Ma of this. I wanted them both to know that Noemi was only my sister in blood. We shared parents; nothing else. We didn't share anything, except for the occasional walk back and forth to school. Even then, we weren't really together. I didn't know what Ma's talking about because I didn't know the Noemi she wanted me to know. I didn't know her at all.*

Then

The girls quietly walked through the night, only their breathing and the occasional car horn breaking the silence. LED lights from several businesses and the sporadically working street lights revealed their shadows tarrying behind them, never catching up. Jasmin's plan was to never talk to Noemi ever again and to never go to the movies again. How could she leave her alone? What would she have told Ma had Noemi returned and Jasmin wasn't there? What then? This was the most dangerous thing that she'd ever done.

Ma's car was parked in the middle of the driveway when they arrived home. Lights from the living room bled onto the driveway.

"Don't snitch," Noemi commanded.

Jasmin rolled her eyes. She had no favor left from Jasmin. None.

"The movie took that long?" Ma asked through clenched teeth. "What did you watch, *Gone With The Wind*?"

"*Gone With The Wind*?" Noemi turned her back towards Ma and mouthed.

"Night, Ma," Jasmin kissed Ma on her cheek.

"Don't *night-Ma* me," Ma scolded. "I feel like I asked you girls to get an earlier movie so that you wouldn't be home at this late hour, but instead you let me beat you home!"

"It wasn't our fault, Ma," Noemi quickly answered.

She was right. It wasn't *their* fault. It was all hers. She was the one who left Jasmin, went with a stranger, and didn't return until hours later. She knew all along what her plan was. Jasmin chewed the inside of her bottom lip, anything to keep from allowing words to leave her mouth. Jasmin hung her head, ashamed. She blamed herself for not knowing what was going to happen. All the signs were there. With Noemi allowing her to choose the movie, wiping away her search history and her outfit! Looking at her now, one would not be able to tell that she had an entire wardrobe change.

"It wasn't?" Ma asked, her face fixed as though to say *yeah right, then whose was it?* She waited for Noemi to start with an explanation because Jasmin's lips were zipped.

"Nah," Noemi continued. "We got to the movie early just like you told us to."

"And?" Ma leaned over the island in the kitchen and rested her chin on her closed fist like she was about to hear the best story ever.

"When we got there, they had just finished wet vacuuming the whole theater and didn't want us to go in at least for another hour. It smelled nice too, like they were using Fabuloso. Ask Jaz!" The words effortlessly rolled off her tongue.

Jasmin bit the inside of her lip some more and swallowed what she hoped was just saliva. She wanted no part of this. *Wet vac? Really?*

"It's about time they clean that place out," Ma remarked. "Glad they finally did."

"Me too!" Noemi agreed. "We weren't the only ones there either. There were a bunch of other folks waiting for the floor to dry; it was starting to get crowded. Since the wait wasn't too long, we figured we'd walk around the mall for the hour."

"That's still late," Ma suggested. "You know I don't like when you girls are out late like this."

"I know, Ma," Noemi weaved her tale. "But when we got back from walking around the mall, which was so boring by the way because we could not afford any of those things that we wanted so we just window shopped." Noemi caught her breath then continued, "I even got Jaz to try on a dress for Homecoming. That's if we go. But the floor was still wet so we had to wait just a little bit more."

Jasmin swallowed hard. She hadn't said anything about homecoming and she certainly wasn't planning to go.

"A dress?" Ma chimed.

"Yeah, Ma," Noemi continued. "She looked really good too."

Just great. A dress is all she heard. She didn't wonder why the movie theater would be wet vacuumed during peak movie watching time. If Jasmin owned a movie theater, she'd make sure she did all her cleaning when she couldn't lose money, when the theater was closed. But, it wasn't her story, not her tale to tell.

"How much was it?" Ma asked. "What store?"

"You do not want to know," Noemi shook her head.

"Did *you* like it?" Ma asked Jasmin.

What was she supposed to say? Could she say that Noemi left her in the movies by herself? She couldn't even say what the movie was about because she was worried about Noemi. She couldn't say any of this, not without getting in trouble herself. Noemi had already dragged her into Act Two of her play, and there was no way for her to escape at this point. Jasmin felt like lies were bowling pins, tightly standing together. For one lie to work, the others would have to fall in line. She didn't think she had the energy or even the brain capacity to handle one pin, let alone the other nine pins.

"Well, Ma, Noemi," Jasmin paused contemplating telling Ma the full story.

Noemi's eyes all but popped out of her head staring at her.

If I tell her, will she believe me? If she believes, will she blame me for not letting her know sooner? Questions plagued her until she finally submitted, "It was okay." The words carefully left Jasmin's mouth. She couldn't even remember a time that she actually liked a dress, not on her anyway.

"Okay?" Noemi feigned. "You wouldn't even be able to tell that it was frumpy old Jaz."

At least that wasn't a lie. If anyone claimed to have ever seen Jasmin in a dress, they wouldn't recognize her.

"I wish I'd been there." Ma stroked Jasmin's hair. It felt warm and comforting. "Did you at least enjoy the movie?"

"Yeah, it was good," Noemi answered before Jasmin could. "I let her choose this time, Ma."

"Good," Ma said, pleased.

"I know she hates musicals so I wanted her to choose whatever she wanted and although it wasn't my favorite, I let my dear sister have her way," Noemi crooned.

"Next time, I'll come along," Ma promised. "It looks like you girls had fun, even though you stayed out too late. Let's try not to do that again. Be careful with the time or at least call the theater to make sure nothing like this happens again."

Noemi draped her arm around Jasmin. Jasmin flinched, not expecting her touch, not liking her touch, not trusting her. She created that story entirely too easily, forcing Jasmin to be a part of it. So that Jasmin didn't lose Ma's trust, she was stuck, stuck with this lie forever.

"Yeah," Jasmin forced a smile.

"Good night, Ma." Noemi released Jasmin, then kissed Ma.

She headed up the stairs leaving Jasmin and Ma there in the kitchen. The whistle of the kettle echoed loudly through the air.

"Tea, Jasmin?" Ma asked.

"No, thank you, ma'am," Jasmin answered. "Ma?"

"Yes?" Ma replied.

"I don't know how to say this, but..." Jasmin fidgeted, avoiding Ma's eyes.

"Say it, hun," Ma slid into the seat next to hers.

"I don't want you to be mad," Jasmin hesitated.

"You know," Ma said. "When I was younger, I didn't have anybody to talk to, not like you and Noemi have me."

"Yeah," Jasmin grunted.

"You could tell me anything," Ma draped her arm around Jasmin's shoulder. "Anything at all."

Jasmin felt the warmth of her mother's love. She felt like she could tell her anything but not everything. She wasn't certain and uncertainty was not safe. "School's hard," Jasmin finally said.

"Life's hard," Ma removed her arm from Jasmin's shoulder stroking her hair instead. "This is the easy part."

"Yeah," Jasmin agreed. "This is the easy part."

This wasn't going to work, not now anyway. She had to figure out a way for Ma to figure this out on her own, maybe catch Noemi in action. This wasn't her job. She wasn't a parent. Why should she concern herself with this? If Noemi wanted to end up on an episode of *Law and Order*, let her.

"Goodnight, Ma." Jasmin finally said escaping from what could've possibly made her night worse.

"Goodnight, sweetheart." Ma answered.

Jasmin took the stairs two by two in a rush to go to bed. Jasmin felt that this wasn't the end though; it was going to return to bite them. Isn't that how the world worked?

"Thanks." Noemi sat at the edge of Jasmin's bed.

Jasmin dressed for bed without a word.

"I said, 'Thanks.'" She reiterated.

In bed, Jasmin engulfed herself with the comforter trying to form some sort of human taco where no part of her body showed. Noemi placed her hand on Jasmin's foot and lightly squeezed her ankle. If her foot hadn't been covered by the comforter, Jasmin imagined that her hand was cold as ice.

"Come on, Jaz," she coaxed. "You're really not going to talk to me?"

Jasmin stiffened and played dead like a possum deterring its prey.

"This was just one thing I had to do," she explained.

Really? Jasmin thought.

"I needed to get it done," she continued. "Plus I wasn't even gone that long."

It took everything Jasmin had not to kick her off the edge of her bed. Jasmin laughed a little because she imagined her falling and getting back up to lunge at her. That wasn't going to end well, so Jasmin kept her thoughts and her kicking leg to herself.

No one should leave their sister, alone, with no explanation. No one should do that. But, Jasmin didn't say that though because by saying that, she'd have to break her vow of silence. Like a Trappist monk, she wasn't going to lift her tongue to utter a word. Not to Noemi. Not ever.

Now

Ma and Jasmin rode home in silence. Thankfully, every light was green and they didn't sit, awkwardly, waiting for them to move forward. On their street it was quiet, just the usual cars on the side of the road rather than in their driveways or garage, where they were supposed to be. No kids were walking across the street, forcing Ma to brake unexpectedly. Ma pulled into their driveway seamlessly. She sat and sighed unusually loud as though releasing an angst of energy.

"Ma?" Jasmin asked. "You alright?" Jasmin knew the answer to this question but asked anyway in hopes of breaking the silence that threatened to stifle them in the car.

Ma sighed again and gripped the steering wheel with both hands, each finger losing its vibrant color as it wrapped tightly around the wheel to create fists.

"Lord, Jesus," Ma cried out. "Please let my daughter be inside when I walk in."

When WE walk in, Jasmin wanted to add but instead, she waited for instructions. She wanted Noemi to be home too, for this to be over. She didn't want to see Ma looking worried.

They left the car, both heavy with hope, Jasmin hoping that she wasted time at the police station, time she could've been using to do homework, read, watch T.V. *This really seemed like something seen on TV. stuff*, Jasmin thought. *Is Noemi's face going to be on a billboard too? Amber Alert? Noemi Alert? Is this the same thing?*

Does Noemi fit the Amber Alert criteria? Is she too old? So, they were both there, hoping that the visit was all in vain. They were going to walk in the house and Noemi was going to start some cockamamie story that Ma will believe because she was just so glad to see her.

Lights streamed out the window and a faint shadow moved about.

"Noemi," both Jasmin and Ma gasped in unison.

They hastened their steps, almost to a jog. Ma turned the knob. She didn't even use her key, as though Noemi would leave the door unlocked. But Ma turned the knob and the door opened.

"Dee?" Ma asked, surprisingly. Uncle Dee sat on the couch with both feet stretched out on Ma's glass center table. There was an opened, black foam container with a mix of chicken bones and uneaten chicken.

"Grace?" Uncle Dee scrambled to sit up, quickly taking his feet from where he knew they shouldn't be. Jasmin shuddered to think about what else he did when he thought no one else was looking. "What you doing here?"

"Noemi here?" Ma asked, heading up the stairs without waiting for an answer.

"No," Uncle Dee told the air, because Ma was out of earshot.

"You haven't seen her at all?" Jasmin asked hopefully.

"Naw," Uncle Dee scratched his head and raised an eyebrow. "She ain't with you?"

Of course, she's not with us, Jasmin wanted to say. *That's why Ma is frantically looking for her and I'm asking you questions.* Jasmin wanted to say this but instead, she said, "No, she's not with us."

"Where's she at?" Uncle Dee asked.

"That's what we're trying to find out."

"You check the school?"

Jasmin didn't answer. Who was going to be at school at this time? But, it wasn't a bad idea. Last place should be the best place to look, right?

Jasmin took the stairs, two by two. Her breath threatened to leave her but she also wanted to tell Ma that checking school would be a good idea. Why not, right? Noemi's door was wide open, and Ma sat on the edge of her bed cradling one of her decorative pillows, one of the small ones not used for sleeping. Jasmin didn't own any because they were a waste of time, but they were all over Noemi's bed, making her room look like a princess's.

"Ma," Jasmin plopped down next to her. "We can go to the school to see if she's-"

"But you said you walked home together," Ma interrupted. "She should be here."

Jasmin remembered that she did say that they walked home together. Knowing Ma's not home after school, Jasmin and Noemi usually went their separate ways, Noemi to rehearsal, track practice, and Jasmin home. They had a routine that worked. Was working? Worked?

"Yeah, but..." Jasmin fumbled her words, "we can still look."

"This just don't make no type of sense," Ma shook her head.

"It doesn't," Jasmin agreed. Noemi should've been there, in her room, yelling at her to get out.

"Why y'all just sitting here?" Uncle Dee bursted into Noemi's room.

"We're going to the school," Ma stated like she just thought of the idea. "Stay here just in case she comes back."

"You know, Grace," Uncle Dee said, "if you'd given these girls phones, we could've tracked her down by now."

Jasmin's eyes widened when he said this. Yes, Jasmin wanted a phone. Was she even normal without one? She and Noemi were probably the only two teenagers on the entire planet without cellphones. Was this the right time to bring this up though? *Read the room, guy,* Jasmin thought.

"Really?" Ma asked, her voice a high pitch.

Jasmin knew this tone. It increased by octaves depending on how mad she was. This was almost at dishes-left-in-the-sink-octave.

"Yeah," Uncle Dee didn't back down. "A phone would've eliminated all of this."

"This is not the time, Dee," Ma pushed past him. "Just stay here."

Jasmin followed Ma down the stairs trying her best to match her stride. She grabbed her keys and they made a scraping sound almost as though they were screaming they didn't want to go. Jasmin didn't want to go either. She didn't think Noemi was at school but she followed because she already planted the idea in Ma's head. Now, nothing would stop her, certainly not Jasmin.

They were about a twenty-minute walk from school but Ma drove like stop signs didn't mean stop. The main gate was still open, so Ma raced through as though they were not on school property. They violently rushed over the speed bump, forcing their bodies to jerk in their seats. It was a miracle they didn't bump their heads on the roof of the car.

Ma removed her seatbelt before parking the car, as Jasmin hurriedly took hers off too. They both charged from the car as though they were getting ready to pull Noemi from under an anvil.

Get Your Homecoming Tickets Before They Sell Out, the marquee screamed in Titanic orange. Bold and brave, Ma didn't see it.

"Ma," Jasmin said. "I don't think we could just walk up to the school like this."

"Watch me!" she said as though Jasmin issued her a challenge.

Twinkling stars helped the school's light posts guide their path. People scattered around the courtyard, some sitting on the rim of the water fountain, their eyes deeply entrenched in their phones, some carrying their large instruments to practice, some just standing, waiting. Looking at them, Jasmin knew that Uncle Dee was right. They did need a phone. She didn't say this to Ma though because unlike Dee, she could read a room.

"Jaz?" Stephen called out. "Miss Hobson?"

"Stephen," Ma bolted towards him. "Have you seen Noemi?"

"No." One of Stephen's eyebrows lifted itself higher than the other. "No, ma'am."

"Are you sure you haven't seen her," Ma asked as though Stephen would lie to her face.

"No, I haven't." Stephen stared at Jasmin as if to ask, *what's going on?*

Simultaneously, Jasmin widened her eyes and shrugged her shoulders. Just like him, she didn't know anything either. She knew Noemi was not at home where she should be. Jasmin didn't want to say that she was *missing* because uttering those words could make it fact. It was like saying, *I'm gonna fail this test.* If you fail the test, you shouldn't be surprised because you made it happen. So, right now, Noemi was not *missing.* She was just not home.

Then

"Do you have the notes from yesterday?" Stephen asked.

Stephen and Jasmin sat at the kitchen table, his school-issued laptop opened, lights glaring from it, papers strewn around it. Jasmin and Noemi's school-issued laptops were where they should be according to Ma, at school and not in her house. They were confined to the desktop upstairs. Stephen used his hotspot to connect to the Internet so that they could complete their homework. The hotspot was something he showed Jasmin how to use several times but she didn't pay attention because she didn't think she'd ever need it.

French was the foreign language she and Stephen decided that they would learn since they thought it would be easy. They'd both seen a lot of movies believing that the class only required a French accent, but that was not the case. In order to earn their foreign language credits for college, they started their journey early in middle school, but it hadn't gotten any easier. While Jasmin and Stephen passed every French class they had, they still didn't know much more than *je m'appelle Jasmin* and it was too late to switch to another language.

"No," Jasmin searched under the mounds of papers. "You had them."

"Naw," Stephen said, "you took them, remember?"

Jasmin probably did but couldn't remember if she'd left them in the folder in class or if she'd brought them home. They had to present information on a French country. Madame Cherry, pronounced *Sherree* (even though Jasmin suspected the only thing French about her were the baguettes she ate every day), said no one could choose Canada since she'd had her fill of Drake. So, Stephen, in his infinite wisdom of all things French except the language, suggested they research the small Caribbean island of Saint Martin.

"It's okay," Jasmin suggested, "we got this!"

"Sure," Stephen sounded uncertain. But, he got on his computer and clickety clacked the keys. Jasmin turned the pages of the only library book she could find about the tiny island.

Diing, Diiing.

The doorbell sounded loud amidst the clickety clacking. Stephen and Jasmin both looked at each other blankly.

"They'll go away," Jasmin suggested.

After turning several pages, the doorbell rang again. Whoever it was, was persistent. Jasmin placed the book on the table, cover up, to save her space, and walked to the door. This was something the librarian advised against as she was convinced it ruined books, but she paid no mind.

Jasmin tiptoed peeping through the hole, twice, just to make sure she saw what she saw?

"Who is it?" Stephen asked.

"Shuhhh," Jasmin hushed Stephen. They both hid behind the door in fear. Maybe if she didn't answer, Jasmin thought, the person at the door would go away. What did he want? Most importantly, how did he even know where she lived?

"What does *he* want?" Stephen whispered after he peeped through the hole.

Jasmin shrugged.

"What are you two doing?" Noemi's callous voice startled them. They hadn't noticed that she'd snuck down the stairs.

"Nothing," Stephen and Jasmin said in unison. Not that they didn't look at all suspicious with both their backs plastered against the door. No, they didn't look suspicious at all. Plus, Ma always said, "don't let nobody in her house that didn't belong there." And, he certainly didn't belong there.

"Move!" Noemi commanded.

They both stiffened. With all four feet firmly planted, their backs became permanent door fixtures.

"Move!" Noemi growled. "Now!"

Jasmin and Stephen split like a hotdog bun preparing for the hotdog sausage.

Noemi opened the door wide without even a glimpse at the peephole. They both knew to first check the peephole. They weren't supposed to open the door to strangers. Even if Barack Obama knocked, he was still a stranger and therefore couldn't enter. Boys were definitely not permitted at *Maison de la Hobson*. Noemi opened the door for both a stranger and a boy.

"Hey," Noemi's growl transformed into a purr.

"Hey," Jah's voice sounded strong and smooth all at the same time. He and all of his six-foot-plus stature entered the house.

If you did not know Jah, then it meant you didn't attend Spring Park High School; you didn't watch local news; and you most definitely lived under a rock. Jah Morat was slated to go pro straight out of high school. The NBA was already calling him and everyone knew it.

"Noemi," Jasmin tugged. "What is he doing here?"

Noemi melted into his embrace like a drop of rain dissolving into the ocean. Jah scooped her up with both his tattooed filled arms close enough so that their lips could greet each other. Jasmin and Stephen looked at each other wide-eyed and trespassing on their obviously intimate exchange. Jasmin heard Jah Morat had a girlfriend, but didn't think it was Noemi. Both girls knew that Ma's rules didn't allow for "boyfriends." Plus, how did they meet? She couldn't imagine Jah at the track or theater. They were both in the same grade but that didn't mean that you'd be in the same class with others of your grade, never mind in class with one of the most attractive, talented, and most, literally... everything, really kids. It wasn't as if they could tell a counselor, "Put me in all the same classes as Jah Morat." At least Jasmin didn't think that was how it worked.

He fit the script for everything. The auburn tips of his dreadlocks stood proudly at the crown of his head while the others relaxed on his shoulder. He even had nice hair. To be honest, he and Noemi looked like the perfect... everything, Jasmin thought.

"What are you doing here?" Words surprisingly left Jasmin's mouth like she was accustomed to talking to him directly. Seeing him on T.V. interviews or watching him float through the courtyard did not do him any justice. He was just as strikingly handsome as those few other times Jasmin was privileged to see him. Except, he was in her house, right in front of her, and she could physically touch him if she wanted to, not that she was a crazy fan.

"Yeah," Stephen chimed in. "What are you doing here?"

"Jah," Noemi crooned. "Don't mind them. Step Hen and my lil sis was just about to continue minding their own business."

"This is my business, and don't call him that," Jasmin quietly demanded. Her squeaking words didn't give the forceful impact she thought they would.

"It really isn't," Noemi hissed. She hooked her arm in Jah's like they were getting ready to walk down an aisle. Instead, they made their way upstairs.

Was she serious? Stephen and Jasmin stood stupefied. What if Ma came home? What were they supposed to do then?

Now

"Where else could she be?" Ma looked at Jasmin and Stephen but the question floated in the air hanging on for no answer. In the main courtyard of the school were only a few kids straggling, some, who weren't deeply trapped in their phones. No one wanted to stop and talk to Ma, Jasmin, or Stephen. Everyone ignored each other.

"Ma," Jasmin said.

Ma pulled out a small piece of paper, an image of Noemi, similar to the one that she had given the detective. How many pictures of Noemi did she have in her wallet?

"Hi," Ma said to a blonde girl, her bangs hanging as she stared at her phone.

"What?" Her gruff voice didn't match the softness of her skin.

Ma gave a half smile, showed her the picture, and asked, "have you seen Noemi?"

"No," the girl grunted and her eyes dropped back to her phone.

"You didn't even look," Ma accused.

Stephen gave Jasmin a worried look, but Jasmin was worried too. They were on school grounds. It didn't matter what time it was. The fact was, they were there, stopping kids, asking questions. It felt like there was a different way to go about this, not this "sort of" violation. She'd seen people escorted from school property. Though this wasn't during school hours, she didn't want to see that happen to Ma. Besides, they still had to attend school here, regardless whether they questioned their friends or not. These were not. Jasmin didn't know these people, but, if she wanted to be remembered, this wasn't how.

Jasmin cautiously touched Ma, guiding her away from the girl's path. Oblivious, the girl sidestepped Ma and continued walking while staring at her phone. Jasmin almost wished that the girl would trip and fall for talking to Ma like that.

"Why'd you do that?" Ma asked.

"Ms. Hobson," Stephen came to Jasmin's rescue. "People here don't care. You definitely don't want to take them away from their phones."

And it was a hard reality but he was right. They did not care. While there were all sorts of charitable projects that students did as a school, they were masked as competitions: canned food drive, coat drive, Thanksgiving drive, Christmas drive. Classes competed to see who could contribute the most and the winners always got something. The coat collection drive, that was a competition. Recycling, that was a competition. Jasmin couldn't even think of something that has ever been done there with only helping in mind. So, Stephen was right. No one there cared.

Ma looked around. Her face was a mixture of confusion and shock. It looked like she got it but then she said, "Why are these kids here so late?" She looked around in disbelief. "And why isn't Noemi here with them? If she's not home, she should be here right? Right?"

"I don't know, Ma."

"She has rehearsals," Ma calculated. "She should be here. On campus."

"I don't know, Ma,"

"Where's the auditorium? Is that where the rehearsal is?" Ma rattled off question after question. "It's around here, right?"

"It may be in the theater teacher's classroom," Jasmin said because the auditorium showed no signs of lights. There was no way that Noemi was there.

"Where's that?" Ma asked.

"I don't know," Jasmin said.

"Do you know anything?" Ma scowled.

"I know where it is," Stephen rescued Jasmin again. He knew that Ma didn't mean to be this way towards Jasmin where she was talking harshly. This was not the Ma he knew.

"Why are you here, Stephen?" Ma asked and now Stephen began to exist again.

"D & D and MC club," Stephen said proudly. But, Noemi said no one should be proud to be a part of that "geek loser" club. Besides, all clubs were made up. Someone decided to meet up as Christians: FCA. Someone decided that they wanted to meet with others to build robots: Robotic club. She said that he shouldn't tell anyone that he was a nerd. *Says.* She *says.*

"Other clubs must be meeting as well, no?" Ma's words hung suspended in the air but neither knew the answer. She passed the water fountain and the large golden lion standing on its hind legs, paws in the air. Jasmin never knew if the lion was getting ready to give a high five or pounce. Stephen and Jasmin followed her as though Ma was the best guide for the school. She wasn't. She hadn't been to the school in a long time, and had never been past the auditorium where Noemi's plays were held.

There had never been a need for her to be at school, besides Noemi's performances. The girls weren't the *I'm-calling-your-parents'* kids. Jasmin and Noemi avoided trouble;

nothing got Ma there and not working. Besides, who else would poor grades or trouble hurt? Nobody but themselves. That was what Ma said anyway. Ma was right, so they did what she asked, went to school, got an education, kept their heads down and out of trouble. *I guess I should now add, 'don't disappear' to this list,* Jasmin thought.

A bank of glass doors blocked their path. Propped open in the daytime and at lunch, students flooded through them like a frightened herd of elephants hunting for food and a possible place to sit. Jasmin usually ended up at a table with Stephen and his D & D buddies. It was not ideal, but it allowed her to eat in an upright position rather than standing because all the tables were taken. Sometimes, they were empty, they just knew that they couldn't sit at a certain table, space or not. For instance, Jasmin knew she couldn't sit at the table with the cheerleaders. She was not a cheerleader. She couldn't sit with the orchestra kids. She didn't play a stringed instrument, or any instrument. Sitting with Stephen and his group was most likely the best spot for her. They didn't judge and they didn't turn her away.

Ma pulled on one of the locked doors. She tried another, then another. She looked at Jasmin as though to ask if she had a key. She didn't. Why would she?

"Why are they locked?" Ma pulled on another door as if she expected it to open magically. Jasmin wanted to tell her that this was not one of those things they shouldn't give up on. Ma always told them to go for what they wanted. *Don't give up. Keep trying.* This was not one of those things. These doors weren't going to magically unlock. In fact, if she kept pulling on them the way she was, it was likely an alarm would sound and they would be seeing the police again.

"Ma," Jasmin said. "There's nothing back there."

Ma put both her palms on her face to create a human binocular and pressed her face to the door. Jasmin did it too, but saw nothing. It was pitch dark on the other side, not even a shadow moved about, no leaves falling. No one was using a skateboard to jump over the outside cafeteria tables. Jasmin imagined how it must be, to be able to sit wherever she wanted during lunch but then reality hit because the only way she could do that was at night time. No one ate lunch at night!

Jasmin looked around surreptitiously. No one wanted their mother at school embarrassing them, especially not in high school, but no one was paying attention. No one was looking. No one was looking at this grown woman with two kids peeking through the locked doors of the cafeteria.

"What now?" Jasmin asked. What were they going to do to move forward? So Jasmin asked. She asked, hoping that Ma knew what to do next because she didn't.

"What now?" Ma's voice was calm and Jasmin didn't know whether she should be afraid or worried, so she decided to give them both the same amount of energy. "We go home."

"Good," Jasmin said. "We can wait. That's what they say on T.V."

"Oh no," Ma shook her head. "We're not waiting. We've got to find her. Waiting does no good. Waiting won't help me find her."

Then

"Your sister is a trip," Stephen said, "fearless even."

"I guess," Jasmin said. *More like selfish*, she thought. She didn't say that Ma catching a boy in the house, let alone in any of their rooms, was a death sentence for them both. But Stephen knew. He knew what Ma was like. Soon, this would not be about Noemi having a boy in the house, but about why Jasmin let Noemi bring a boy in the house. Or, why didn't Jasmin call Ma with the boy in the house? Somehow, this would all fall back on Jasmin.

One time they were all sitting down to dinner at the kitchen table: Jasmin, Uncle Dee, Noemi, Stephen and Ma. Ma, a rare occasion, had made them dinner. The scent of melted cheese from the baked macaroni greeted their nostrils so they knew it would be a good night. With only broccoli left on Jasmin's plate, the doorbell rang. They all looked up; no one was expecting guests.

"Ignore them," Ma said. "And they'll go away."

They did, but the doorbell rang again. This forced Ma to leave her unfinished dinner to answer the door.

"How can I help you?" Ma used her *I-don't-know-you-yet* voice, the voice that people got before she figured out how she needed to be. All they heard was Ma's side of the conversation, riddling off a bunch of questions. "Who? What do you want? Why? What do you want with her? Who are you? Who are you parents? Where do you live? Around here? Why have I never seen you?"

Uncle Dee took a bite of his Mac and cheese then walked to the door. He quickly joined the inquisition. "How'd you get this address? Who told you that you could come here?"

Eventually, Stephen and Jasmin also went to the door leaving Noemi at the table. She didn't eat. Swirling her fork around her half empty plate, she moved the food from one area of the plate to the next. She did that sometimes when she didn't want to finish her food. Nevertheless, Stephen and Jasmin went. When they got to the door, a beanstalk of a boy stood on the outside. Inside, he'd probably towered over Uncle Dee. His legs barely held him up. With his eyes widely opened, his hands hid in his pockets. Little beads of sweat ran down his forehead.

"I just..." he swallowed, "wanted to say hi to Noemi."

"For what?" Uncle Dee asked. "How do you know her?"

"We're in the same class."

"She told you that you could come here?" Uncle Dee asked, then stated, "I know she didn't tell you to come here."

"No, I just thought," the boy answered.

"You just thought, what, that you'd just show up at grown people's house to ask for their daughter?" Uncle Dee snapped.

"Yeah," the boy answered, his eyes glued to his feet.

"Yes, sir," Uncle Dee demanded.

"Yes, sir," the boy repeated.

Stephen and Jasmin didn't know who he was because Noemi was already in the 9th grade at that time, in a totally different school. Jasmin thought that he'd been bold enough to go to a girl's house and not just any girl's house, but Noemi's whose Ma was Ma.

"You see enough of her at school," Uncle Dee suggested. "Talk to her there."

"Matter of fact," Ma added. "Don't say nothing to my daughter, when you see her, don't even speak."

"Yeah," Uncle Dee added.

Eventually, Ma called, "Noemi, come here."

Noemi walked slowly to the door like Jasmin imagined someone on death row would walk to their execution, slowly and fearfully. Stephen and Jasmin parted so that she could stand between Ma and Uncle Dee but directly in front of the boy who had sweated buckets by this time.

"Yes, Ma?" Noemi hung her head.

"Look at me, girl, when I'm talking to you," Ma demanded. "You know this boy?"

"Yes, Ma."

"You invited him here?"

"No, Ma," Noemi whispered.

"How'd he get our address then?"

Noemi shrugged her shoulders.

"Use your words, Noemi." Ma scolded.

"I don't know, Ma," Noemi answered.

"You don't know, huh?" Ma stared at Noemi. "You don't know? He's here to see you. Not me. Not Dee. Not Stephen. Not Jasmin, but you."

"The audacity," Uncle Dee sneered.

"Yes, the audacity," Ma agreed. Ma then slammed the door shut so hard that it echoed throughout the house.

That night, Ma accused them both of having people over when she was gone. She suggested that this was something that the girls did often when she wasn't there. Now, she could no longer trust them. Jasmin thought that this was unfair, of course, because like Ma'd pointed out, the mysterious boy hadn't intended to see

Jasmin. Again, Noemi sucked Jasmin into her mess. That was the night that Ma declared that they couldn't have anyone over. "Except you, Stephen." *Harmless*, she called him. This was also the night she said her schedule would no longer be on the refrigerator door. Ma insisted that the girls no longer needed that information, especially when they planned wild parties in her house. Everything was an overreaction with Ma. Easily, an unexpected visit from a boy graduated into wild parties they never had and probably never would.

The reality was that they never really knew her schedule, not after that night. It wasn't written down and posted anywhere. Jasmin's schedule was simple: school, nothing more. Noemi's however filled her school schedule: theater, track practice or performance, times and names emblazoned in different colors. Both their schedules plus the cleaning schedule that Noemi barely ever followed were written on the dry erase board stuck on the refrigerator. Although Noemi's schedule took up the majority of the space, it still allowed room for Ma's, but she didn't write it.

"You still here?" Noemi marched directly to the refrigerator and pulled out a bottle of orange juice. Her shorts were rolled up at her waist making them shorter than they really were. Long, smooth legs that belonged on a runway traipsed through the kitchen.

"Aaah, yeah," Stephen's eyes roamed her body.

"No dork convention tonight that you can take your friend to?" She looked at Jasmin with disgust.

"Noemi," Jasmin whispered so that her voice wouldn't travel up the stairs to the unwanted guest. "You know we're not supposed to have boys here. What if Ma comes home?"

"She won't," Noemi stated.

"You don't know that," Jasmin answered. "We don't even know her schedule."

"He's a boy," Noemi's eyes darted daggers into Stephen. "He's here, right?"

"It's not the same and you know it," Jasmin countered. She knew Stephen was not the type of boy Ma was talking about. They practically grew up with him and besides Ma knew he was there. "If Ma walked in right now, she would not be surprised to see him here. But Mr. Future NBA up there? Ma is going to kill us."

"Ha, ha, ha," Noemi laughed, her voice just short of Cruella's.

"I'm serious, Noemi," Jasmin continued her whisper. "Ma is not going to like this."

"I got a boy here and you got a boy here," she removed two glasses from the dish drainer and filled them both with the juice.

"And you're eating in your room?" Jasmin laughed nervously.

"She's gangsta," Stephen chuckled.

Noemi moved closer to Stephen and lifted his pendant in her palm. His necklace raised up from his skin. "What's in this thing anyway?"

"It's Boba Fett's pendant," Stephen began to explain. "From Star Wa-"

"No one cares," Noemi snapped the pendant and it landed back on Stephen's chest.

It was as if everything happened in slow motion. Suddenly, Jasmin wanted Noemi to leave to not terrorize Stephen the way she liked. Go back upstairs and hope Ma didn't come home right away.

"Noemi," Jasmin begged. "Stop."

"You're a boy!" She dug her index finger into his chest and stared into his face.

Stephen gulped.

"Right?" Noemi questioned.

"Yeah," Stephen finally answered. "But..."

"But, what?" Noemi continued her inquisition. "But you're not sure you're a boy?"

"No," Stephen stuttered.

"No, you're not a boy?" Noemi asked purposely, intending to confuse Stephen.

"That's not what I mean," Stephen struggled. "I'm a boy, but I'm not him."

"No, you're definitely not him," Noemi laughed bitterly.

"Noemi," Stephen said. "All Jaz is saying is that Ms. H is going to be here any minute."

"You don't know that," Noemi declared.

"You don't know that she won't," Jasmin added.

"Plus," Stephen continued. "Ms. H knows I'm here."

"So what?" Noemi proceeded. "So, you're here. How's that fair?"

"Ms. Hobson...," Stephen uttered.

"Step Hen," Noemi leaned in further, her face mere inches away from his. "Ms. Hobson is not here."

The lump in Stephen's throat moved up then down. His cheeks hardened.

"Who's going to tell her?" Noemi asked. "You?"

"No," Stephen finally found his voice after what seemed like a long time.

"You?" She looked at Jasmin without moving away from Stephen.

"No," Jasmin submitted.

"Then, we're all good here." She moved away from Stephen and grabbed both glasses.

"Noemi," Jasmin pleaded. "I don't like this."

"I like it," she admitted. "I like it a lot."

"We don't know when Ma's coming home," Jasmin reminded her. "It could be any time now."

"Or," Noemi offered. "It could be no time now."

"Do you at least have a plan?" Jasmin asked. "What do we say if she does come home now?"

"She won't."

"But, what if she does?" Jasmin asked again.

Stephen stayed silent, his eyes back and forth from Jasmin to Noemi like watching a tennis match.

"You worry too much, little sis," Noemi pointed out. "Mostly, about stuff that don't even concern you."

"This concerns me, Noemi."

"How?" She put the glasses back on the counter. "How exactly does *this* concern you?"

She knew exactly how her having a boy in her room, in the house, other than Stephen, concerned Jasmin, but didn't care. Granted, Jah was not at the house to see her. He probably didn't even know who she was. While he was Noemi's "guest," they were both going to get punished for something that Jasmin didn't even do. So, yes, this did concern her.

"Noemi, you know Ma is not going to like this, right?" Jasmin asked.

"Jaz," Noemi rolled her eyes. "You're going to die of a stroke."

"You're giving me a stroke," Jasmin answered.

"Ma can't *not like* what she doesn't know, right?" She asked.

"I guess, but..."

"Relax, sis," She patted the top of Jasmin's head as though petting a dog.

Jasmin quickly brushed her hand off, "Don't do that."

"Relax," she continued. "Ma's at work. We'll be fine."

"Noemi, he should go now," Jasmin demanded.

"He's staying," she said, matter-of-factly.

"Noemi," Jasmin begged. "If Ma walks in here right now, we're all dead."

"You're overreacting as usual."

"All of us," Jasmin said again, "including your guest, so it's probably best that he leaves."

"Girl, it's not that serious." She grabbed the glasses again and made her way out of the kitchen. "It's not."

Stephen and Jasmin tried to finish their project. They couldn't help but jump every time they heard a car or when lights seeped across the living room. Jasmin began to think that a stroke would probably be easier than Ma walking in and catching this.

But that night, Ma didn't come home so they lived to see another day.

Now

Frustration, anxiety, disappointment, but most of all, confusion filled the car as Ma drove them home, Jasmin riding shotgun, Stephen quietly in the back. Nothing but the sounds of the bottom of the car being dragged against raised concrete, loud and scratchy, filled the car. Each time it scraped, their bodies popped up out of their seats like jack-in-boxes. Each time, Jasmin hoped her head wouldn't hit the roof. They didn't complain though, and rode in silence.

Ma pulled in the driveway and Uncle Dee hung his head back blowing rings of smoke in the air. He then dropped something and used his foot to grind the stub into the concrete.

"Noemi's home?" Ma barely put the car in park before she yelled to Uncle Dee.

He shook his head, no.

"She called?"

Uncle Dee shook his head, no, again.

"This is not like her," Ma mused.

Out of the car, they headed to the house when suddenly Ma turned towards Stephen to say, "You can go home, Stephen. It's late."

"You sure, Ms. H?" Stephen pulled out his cell phone. "I can call my parents right now and let them know I'm needed here."

"Thanks, but it's ok, really," Ma said, dismissing him.

Stephen looked at Jasmin as though she knew what Ma's thinking, but she didn't. Jasmin couldn't help but think about the time at the doctor's office. Ma insisted she wouldn't need an inhaler. "God will breathe for her," Ma told the doctor. With no idea how Jasmin was going to deal with her breathing issues, they left with no inhaler. *This is just like that*, Jasmin thought. *We could use all the help that we can get.*

When someone was missing, *they* usually said that the first twenty-four hours were the most critical. Or was it the first forty-eight hours? Thoughts forced their way in Jasmin's mind, pushing her to not think about the fact that Noemi wasn't there. What did that possibly mean? She didn't want to put her in this "missing" category. But, no other word came to mind; nothing that made sense anyway. Thoughts flooded her mind like a lake after heavy rains. *Most of those girls weren't found, unless...*Jasmin thought. *Unless they were on a T.V. show and even then, there wasn't always a happy ending.*

Jasmin squeezed her eyes shut whispering, "Happy ending. Happy ending." She tried not to think so far ahead, but the thoughts took over like a dictator. "Positive thoughts. Positive thoughts," she whispered again. *She's just out somewhere and got caught up*, Jasmin said to herself. *She's coming home for sure.*

"I'll see you tomorrow, then Jaz," Stephen said, disappearing into the night.

Jasmin wanted to tell Ma to let him stay. They needed to pound the pavement, post pictures, and do whatever was necessary. She wanted to say this; instead, she remained silent. Her chest tightened and she gripped her shirt and squeezed it tightly. *One, two*, she counted and tried to trap the air in her lungs before releasing it. *One. Two. One. Two.* She attempted to clear her mind but the thoughts continued. Worry wouldn't leave her. *We've never been apart this long outside of school. Usually she's in her room, at the table, in the living room, but never away from the house, not without me. While we separate on our walks to and sometimes from school, Noemi always comes home before Ma, so that Ma never knows that we aren't actually doing what she always says for us to do — stay together.*

Jasmin tried to think back. Maybe she missed something. Did Noemi tell her she was going somewhere and she dismissed it? Was that why she was not home yet? Was Jasmin supposed to meet her somewhere and forgot? Jasmin was almost... mostly... positive that Noemi would've said something like, *I'll be late,* or *don't expect me early*. Something to let Jasmin know that she was all right, a cover story just in case this very thing happened.

"Yes, this is an emergency," Ma said as Jasmin walked into the house. She talked on the phone and Uncle Dee was staring at her.

"911," Uncle Dee said. "I told her she's supposed to call the detective directly, but she's not listening."

Uncle Dee was right, not that Noemi's missing status wasn't an emergency but they'd been assigned a detective. Jasmin shuddered to think that they were doing "protocol" for a missing person, her sister. Nothing about this felt real to her, nothing, but they'd already visited the station, a detective's number, a case number. Ma really should've been calling Sanchez directly like Uncle Dee suggested, but instead she was on the emergency line with what was technically a non-emergency.

"Listen to me," Ma raised her voice to why-is-this-kitchen-not-cleaned octave. "This *IS* an emergency."

Jasmin looked at her, concerned. She wanted to remind her of what she always said, "you can catch more flies with honey than with vinegar." Lots of vinegar was pouring out of Ma right now.

Jasmin and Uncle Dee just stood there, stared at Ma, and waited for instructions because there was nothing Ma was going to listen to right now. No talking her out of whatever she was planning. Whether it made sense or not, she was doing it with or without their input.

Jasmin wanted to remind Ma that the detective said to wait, wait for Noemi to call or simply return home. Ma could kill her then. But, she was doing just the opposite.

"Detective Sanchez," Ma said into the phone. "Shawn Sanchez."

Silence.

"No," Ma. continued. "He didn't give me a case number. I don't think."

Jasmin wanted to remind her that they did have a case number but she stayed silent instead.

"Yes," Ma's voice was curt, more vinegar. "I'm sure he didn't give me a case number."

Silence.

Jasmin looked through Ma's purse, the one she cradled throughout their visit to the station. She grabbed the piece of paper with the case number on it and placed it in front of Ma. Ma quickly looked at it, shaking her head then shoving the piece of paper aside.

"Why wouldn't he be in?" Ma asked. "I just spoke with him."

It had been at least two hours since they'd left the station, Jasmin wanted to say. She wanted to say that there were other things detectives had to do. They probably weren't going to drop everything because Noemi didn't know Ma's schedule. It was not Detective Sanchez's fault that Noemi wasn't home. It wasn't the dispatcher's fault either.

"Yes," she said bitterly, "transfer me."

Jasmin wanted her to put the phone on speaker but again, she remained silent because Ma's face was an equal mixture of worry and anger and Jasmin did not want to get caught in the crossfire. While Ma wasn't brandishing a weapon, her words were just as sharp.

Ma paced back and forth as much as the phone's cord allowed. If this was a path in the road, it wouldn't be the path less traveled.

Loud music came out of the receiver, loud enough that Uncle Dee and Jasmin heard. Ma covered the phone's mouthpiece and whispered, "I'm on hold."

"You don't have this guy's number?" Uncle Dee asked.

"This is Ms. Hobson," Ma ignored Uncle Dee, "Grace Hobson. I just left your office, uhm, desk, regarding Noemi Hobson. We checked. She's not at school. Please give me a call back as soon as possible." Ma rattled off their phone number into the phone; said thank you and hung up.

"Where's the card, Grace?" Uncle Dee asked. "I know they gave you one."

"He's going to call back now, right?" Ma ignored Uncle Dee's question and asked her own questions to no one in particular.

"Yes, Ma," Jasmin answered. "I'm sure of it." She wasn't though. She wasn't sure of anything right now. Absolutely nothing made sense. Noemi should be there, at least walk in the house any minute now. She was going to walk in. Ma was going to shout her head off and she was going to punish the both of them. Jasmin would take it though. She'd take the punishment right now, the yelling, if it meant Noemi walking through the door right this minute. But it didn't happen. Noemi didn't walk through the door.

The phone rang and its decibel bursted through Jasmin's thoughts. Ma didn't let it ring more than once though before she answered, "Noemi?"

They all stopped breathing to hope and pray that it was indeed Noemi. They hoped she was stranded somewhere and calling for a ride. Whatever she was doing would be forgiven, just come home.

"No, I am not interested in upgrading my internet," Ma screamed into the phone and slammed it down. It wasn't Noemi. Ma's breath sank. Hope fizzled out of the room like air released from a balloon.

Ma sat on the stool in the kitchen and dug her face into her hands; then her entire body sank in surrender. She began to sob into her hands while her shoulders lifted up and down with each expulsion of breath. Jasmin didn't ever remember a time Ma cried. Even in the face of losing her clients, a tear never left her eyes, no expression. But this, this was not Ma, a broken woman who didn't know where her child was. Jasmin was lost too. What could she do?

Uncle Dee walked to Ma and wrapped his arm around her. "I'm sure she'll be home soon."

More sobs left Ma's body.

"She's a good kid," Uncle Dee reassured. "She probably got caught up somewhere, you know?"

"Where?" Ma whipped her head up. "Why?"

"I don't know, Grace," Uncle Dee said.

"This is not like her," Ma sobbed.

"I know," he agreed.

"She wouldn't just not come home like this."

"I know."

"She's not even at school, Dee," Ma pointed out.

"I know," Uncle Dee rubbed Ma's back. "I know,... I know."

"What we gonna do, Dee?" Ma stared into Uncle Dee's face. Tears joined the snot that ran from her nose.

Jasmin didn't know this woman, not this woman who pleaded with Uncle Dee, not this woman whose face was filled with tears and snot, not this inconsolable woman. This woman both scared and worried Jasmin.

Sleep wasn't going to come tonight, not with Noemi absent.

Then

"I don't want to go," Jasmin ranted as she tried dodging the other kids trying to go home. Angry cars were forced to wait for the sign that said *do not walk*. Kids meandered across the street ignoring every car. The crossing guard rushed them across even though the *do not walk* sign instructed them to stay put. Some students spilled into the streets, the sidewalk unable to contain them.

"We don't have to stay the entire game," Noemi coaxed. "and you can even bring Step Hen."

Cars crawled by, some blew their horns. Still, students walked in the streets as if they owned it, the crossing guard no help to the motorists. She looked frustrated and defeated. The "don't walk" sign continued to blink. No one waited for the little man to tell them to go.

"Stop calling him that," Jasmin demanded. "I'm not even a little bit interested in watching this stupid game."

"Where's your school spirit, huh?" Noemi persisted.

"School spirit?" Jasmin scoffed. "When did *you* get school spirit?" As far as Jasmin knew, Noemi was never interested in showing school spirit. She didn't cheer when they won championships, and they won a lot of those according to the school news that they forced them to watch each morning. She didn't go to the pep rallies unless they were mandatory. She didn't even wear school colors on spirit days. She almost ignored her own track meets. Who was this new person who was interested in supporting her school, in showing school spirit? She was new to Jasmin.

"Com'on," she coaxed.

"What if Ma comes home?" Jasmin asked, mostly her main concern. What about Ma? Not concerned about her safety, about transportation, about what they'd eat, none of that superseded her concern over Ma. "How do we explain that? We didn't even ask her to go anywhere. You know she needs to know where we are at all times."

"We'll tell her I had emergency rehearsals. Show's starting soon and Ms. Bitters wanted us to run through some things," Noemi moved closer to Jasmin wrapping her arm around so that they walked awkwardly among the crowd.

"Ma's not going to believe that," Jasmin answered. "Shoot, I don't believe that."

"Why wouldn't she," Noemi's grip tightened around Jasmin's frail body. She may as well have tied both their legs together as though in a three-legged race.

"Right," Jasmin said reluctantly, shoving Noemi's arm from her shoulders. Her arm felt like Jasmin imagined ice felt in hot water, unnatural. "But I'm still not interested."

They both knew that Noemi only seemed this cooperative when she wanted something from Jasmin. Her charm was never without cause, never without reason. Sadly, Jasmin was used to her behavior by now. When she wanted something, she'd speak to Jasmin in public, otherwise she would ignore her. At school, Noemi and her friends passed by Jasmin as though they weren't sisters, as though they didn't sleep one door away from each other.

There were several snags with this plan. Jasmin wasn't interested in watching any game, never been interested and she wasn't going to suddenly become interested. Who wanted to see a bunch of kids run up and down a court just to put a ball in a basket? Stupid. Jasmin also wanted to avoid other students too, as mingling during classes was more than enough. She couldn't even imagine being around them without adult supervision. If they behaved like a bunch of jackasses during class with a teacher, what would it be like without? Jasmin didn't want to have to suffer that. Plus, it was probably going to be a loud and disgusting crowd, not something she wanted to do, ever. She was certain Stephen felt the same. They'd never attended any gatherings, no games, no parties. Besides Stephen's gaming club, they once in a while had lunch in the cafeteria. Stephen and Jasmin weren't like Noemi who had her theater group who it seemed everyone knew. Plus, what if Ma came home? She'd be mad they weren't there.

"So," Noemi interrupted Jasmin's thoughts.

"So?" Jasmin pretended as though she had no idea what Noemi had said.

"Com'on, Jazzi pooh," she gushed. She was really piling it on. This must've been a really special game.

"Naw," Jasmin said. "I got work to do. Lots of it."

"You know, if you keep living this way," she warned. "You're going to end up..."

"End up what?" Jasmin interjected. "With an education? Freedom? Choices?"

"Well, yeah, but," Noemi used her key to open the door.

Jasmin hadn't realized they'd gotten home so quickly, "end up with a really good job?"

"I guess," Noemi threw her bag on the living room's floor. "If that's all you want out of life."

"What else is there?"

"Are you serious right now," she chuckled. "You gotta get out and meet people, get involved in school, hang out."

"I do all of that, Jasmin answered.

"I'm not talking bout with Step Hen," Noemi rolled her eyes.

"You've got to get involved in school. There is so much that you're missing out on,"

"I doubt it," Jasmin disagreed.

"Ok," Noemi suggested. "This is also a chance for us to spend time together."

"Really?" Jasmin mocked heading directly to the refrigerator. It always felt like they walked through the desert walking home from school. It was so hot. But, why would Noemi even want to spend time with Jasmin? Why now?

"Yeah," she somehow managed to drape her arm around Jasmin again. "I'll be going off to college soon."

"Ok."

"Moments like these will be harder for us to find, you know?" Her voice was as soft as a marshmallow. "Plus, Ma always says we've got to enjoy the time we've got, especially since it's just us."

Noemi took a bottle of water from the refrigerator and handed it to Jasmin. Jasmin eyed her suspiciously.

"I guess," Ma always said that, not that they ever actually ever did. Although they were so close to each other, they were still very far apart, nothing they liked about each other. All they shared: DNA, residence, school and Uncle Dee, made them unlike sisters, at least the sisters Jasmin had seen on T.V.

Jasmin thought about the twin sisters at her school, the ones in her grade. Every time she saw one, she saw the other. Jasmin didn't even know which was Evelyn or which Emma. Matter of fact, she didn't think her teachers could tell them apart either. Sometimes, they held hands, not that Jasmin wanted her and Noemi to hold hands, but she did yearn for a relationship. Instead Noemi spoke to her only when she wanted something. She yearned for a real relationship, a relationship so real that whenever people saw them, they'd suggest they star on their own "sisterhood" reality show. Suddenly an anger swelled up in Jasmin and she said, "you're just gonna leave me again like you always do. I'm not falling for this."

"Why would I ever do that?" Noemi smiled, avoiding Jasmin's eyes.

"Right," Jasmin sighed. "Why would you?"

"Look," Noemi said firmly. "I'd never do that again. Promise."

"Promise?" Jasmin laughed. "Your promises are as useless as a dead battery. You're not doing that to me again."

"Jaz," Noemi cooed. "Think about it. We're on school property. Where am I gonna go?"

"Who knows," Jasmin responded coldly.

"You know what?" Noemi threw up her arms in surrender, "if you don't want to spend time with me, you don't have to. Whatever."

Where's she gonna go, Jasmin tried to reason with herself. *The game's on campus. It's after school and nothing else is going on. Maybe she does want to spend time with me.* "Ok," Jasmin submitted.

"So, you'll go," Noemi exclaimed.

"Sure," Jasmin said, hoping she'd made the right decision.

Noemi flung both arms around Jasmin's neck pulling her closer. She kissed Jasmin sloppily on her cheek.

"Yuck," Jasmin quickly wiped off her cheek with the back of her hand. She was right though, Jasmin thought. *We do need to spend more time together because any minute, she'll be gone.* Jasmin hadn't really thought about it much, her being gone, all the way to a college dorm room that wasn't one door away from hers. She'd be out of the house, probably out of the state. The thought of Noemi's future absence saddened her. Although they weren't Emma and Evelyn, they were still sisters, Jasmin and Noemi, sisters for the rest of their lives, so, why not try to get closer? What would it hurt?

Now

J asmin and Stephen walked in silence, not a word between them, no idle talk to drown the sounds of passing traffic and other students. Stephen didn't even talk about his gaming club. It was clear that something was missing. Someone was missing.

Overhanging trees dropped shadows on the street. Lights from cars and a few street lamps illuminated their path. Why was it so dark? Even the stars were asleep. High school began in the dark of night, very different from middle school where at least the sun shone, except for when it rained. Thoughts of Noemi filled Jasmin's mind. *Where could she possibly be? Why wouldn't she come home?*

Vehicle after vehicle crawled by trying not to hit the students. Some were over the crosswalk but kids walked beside them as though they weren't dangerous. As they walked, Jasmin thought of Noemi, certain that she would not be able to think about anything else, not French, not Math, nothing. But, what was she going to do at home? Watch Ma be motionless?

"Have you heard anything from the police yet?" Stephen interrupted her thoughts.

"Naw," Jasmin said. "Nothing. It's like they're not even looking."

"It's not been that long," he stated. "Don't people need to be miss-"

"Noemi's not missing," Jasmin quickly corrected him.

"I mean," he stuttered. "We don't know that, do we?"

"We don't know that she's not not-missing either," Jasmin heard herself say. It sounded better in her head, like she knew what she was saying or what she was talking about. But, she didn't believe what she was saying, so it sounded like nonsense aloud.

"Isn't the procedure," he paused as though he was thinking about what to say next. "I mean, I don't know, Jaz, but isn't there usually a waiting period with these types of things?"

"What types of things? This isn't a *procedural* thing," Jasmin said that word, procedure with all of its syllables so that Stephen knew that *this,* Noemi missing, wasn't just a procedural thing.

"Missing," he cleared his throat. "Noemi not here. Don't the police have to wait twenty-four hours, forty-eight, or something like that?"

"I don't think that it's the same for mis-" Jasmin stopped herself from saying the M word because that was not what this was. Then she told him the story of Ma calling the detective only to get his voicemail. He still hadn't called back.

"How's your mom holding up?" Stephen asked.

"She's good," Jasmin lied because she still didn't know her mother. She didn't tell him that Ma was still at home with dark circles around her eyes and tear stains on her face. She didn't tell him that she left her wearing the clothes that she'd worn the day before. She didn't tell him that Ma's behavior reflected two different women. Jasmin thought, for sure, by now, Ma'd have her own police force looking for Noemi. But, all that fizzled within hours. Her old Ma bear was more like a lost cub.

"Is she really?" He scrunched his eyebrows together. "Because this doesn't seem like the type of situation that she'd be *good* with."

"Yeah," Jasmin lied again. "She is. You know Ma; she can handle anything."

"Why are you even going to school?" he asked.

"Cause if I don't they gonna arrest Ma," Jasmin joked but Stephen didn't laugh. No time for jokes, not with all this stuff, not with Noemi being gone. No. Not here.

They strolled through the gate with the other walkers. There, they tried to avoid the kids in their fancy cars who were speeding. Everyone else drove at a snail's pace to avoid killing pedestrians. Jasmin looked in the direction Noemi usually went when they separated, but she was not there. She wasn't walking ahead of them as usual nor "not-looking back" at them when she was with her friends. Jasmin's eyes began to well up with tears.

"It's ok," Stephen stopped too. "She'll come home. I'm sure of it."

Stephen wrapped one arm around Jasmin, the other hoisting his backpack. Tears dropped from Jasmin's eyes freely, but she hid them in his shirt so no one knew what was really happening. Her body weakened, collapsing into him. Tears flowed like a hydrant now, loosely like an escaped balloon in the skies. *I don't know. I don't know if it's going to be ok. I don't like not knowing,* Jasmin thought.

"Move," someone yelled.

"Y'all just gonna stand there and block everybody?" Yelled another.

Immediately, they were reminded of where they were and Jasmin wondered if she, like Ma, really should've stayed home today.

WHILE JASMIN THOUGHT she couldn't concentrate in any of her classes, in science, she thought would take her mind off of Noemi not at school. Ms Atoms, her Science teacher, always had an activity, something that most kids couldn't keep their eyes off of. No one knew how she did it, but she even made taking notes entertaining. If all Jasmin's classes were like Ms. Atoms, kids probably wouldn't sleep in class. But, today, Ms. Atoms didn't hold her attention.

It was the middle of the day, just before lunch and still no news. Jasmin imagined that they, somebody, anybody would collect her from class to tell her that Noemi's home and there was nothing to worry about. *Is that something they'd do?* she wondered. Maybe they wouldn't think it was that serious. Just another girl returning home after... whatever she was doing.

Jasmin wanted to yell. The minute she got home, she was going to yell all sorts of things at her like how selfish could you be? You didn't even think about anyone but yourself! What about Ma? It had not been twenty four hours yet, but to Jasmin, it felt like days that Noemi had been gone. Jasmin tried to concentrate on the rocks that lined Ms. Atoms' desk as though they created some sort of magical force field. Each had its own personality and grooves, some big, some small, none smooth. Who would line their desks with stones?

"Jasmin?" Ms. Atoms' voice broke her concentration and the rocks released.

Jasmin liked Ms. Atoms. She gave hugs to everyone before entering her classroom, even the toughest looking kids. The ones who everyone knew had been in a lot of trouble, lined up to get one. They were soothing, for the kids. She didn't give those quick one-arm side hugs either, but wrapped both arms around the body holding on for what seemed like decades. Today, Jasmin literally melted in her arms, nestling her head on Ms. Atoms' chest because she somehow knew that was going to make her feel better. It did, for a brief moment.

"Yes, Ms. Atoms?" Jasmin answered.

"You haven't written anything in your notebook baby," she pointed out.

Jasmin looked at her notebook and Ms. Atoms was wrong. She had written something. The vertical and horizontal lines needed to start her notes were written in pencil on the pages. But, Jasmin didn't say this. She didn't say that Ms. Atoms was wrong. She instead stared at the crooked looking cross in her notebook. That was something, right?

"I'm sorry," Jasmin apologized.

"It's ok, baby," Ms. Atoms said. The slide on the board was filled with words that should've been in Jasmin's notebook, and she said it was ok like it really was. "Bell's about to ring, so you'll have to get the notes from the class website," she crooned.

"Ok," Jasmin said, shoving the notebook in her backpack. Everyone followed suit because once Ms. Atoms said the bell was about to ring, it was really code for: teaching is over.

Ms. Atoms' phone rang and she gracefully glided back towards her desk.

"Um huh," Ms. Atoms looked at Jasmin. "She's here, ok, I'll send her."

Jasmin knew that look: either the front office or the Dean's office. She knew this from school procedure. Jasmin was never in trouble, not with another kid, not with a teacher, so, it was not the dean. Ma never picked them up early from school, in order to not miss a good education. Plus in Ma's state this morning, there was no way this could be ...

Unless...

Ms. Atoms put the receiver back in place and walked over towards Jasmin. Every pair of eyes followed her, including Jasmin's. Jasmin swallowed hard and forced herself not to blink. Her chest began to heave like that elephant was coming to sit on it again. *Am I in trouble*, she wondered. *For what though*? Thoughts bounced around her mind like a kangaroo: *I am in trouble. They think I know where Noemi is, but I don't. I don't. Unless...Maybe Ma is coming to get me out of school early. What if it's not for good news though. What if...*

Kids were ready to sing oooh as they normally did when teachers said someone was going to the dean or *lucky* if they were going home.

"Jasmin," Ms. Atoms said softly, aware that everyone was looking at her and now at Jasmin.

"Front office?" Jasmin asked.

"Yes," Ms. Atoms whispered but not soft enough because the *oohs* started. They echoed throughout the classroom as though Jasmin was someone who was ever called to the office.

Jasmin hoisted her backpack over one shoulder walking through the gauntlet of oooohs, down the empty hallway, straight towards the office. Just as she turned the corner, the bell rang and students flooded the hallway on their way to lunch or their next classes. Jasmin had A lunch so if Ma was indeed there to pick her up, she'd miss that. *Oh, no*, Jasmin thought sarcastically but, still she worried about why they called her to the office.

She made her way to the crowd. No one cared that she was in the hallway first and probably deserved the right of way. They pushed and prodded like cattle in a herd. No one cared that she was trying to hurry. Finally, she reached the edge of the hallway where the office was to see Ma was not there to pick her up early. She was not there to tell her that Noemi had returned home and everything was good. Instead, the school's resource officer and Detective Sanchez stood inches above the crowd awaiting her arrival.

Then

N oemi sashayed down the stairs and into the kitchen making each step intentional. Her long legs entered before the rest of her body. Jasmin sometimes wondered why her legs weren't runway-ready like Noemi's. Instead they were stubby like crinkle fries. Jasmin kept Noemi in her peripheral view, careful not to fix her gaze on her. Though she knew that's what Noemi wanted, she continued her English homework underlining the nouns like Ms. Perez told them. It wasn't due for another few days but what else was Jasmin going to do with all her free time? Getting ahead in homework seemed the wise choice.

Hope
Thing
Feathers
Soul

Jasmin underlined these words in her notebook pretending not to notice Noemi's long legs oozing out her very short shorts. She wore those same shorts that revealed the insides of her pockets, the ones Jasmin knew Ma hadn't bought. _What a waste of space_, Jasmin thought. _Pockets that you can't use._

Bird
Land

Noemi topped it off with an oversized sweatshirt. This was a source of confusion for Jasmin because girls at school wore the largest, most oversize sweaters over their shorts. Sometimes they were so big that anyone could be fooled to think that they weren't wearing shorts, nothing but the sweater. They acted like Florida didn't have only two seasons, hot and hotter. Noemi, like all girls, acted as though the weather wasn't as hot as boiling water outside. Although she wanted to, Jasmin didn't say anything. She didn't ask where she got the pants from like she wanted to. She wanted to say they were too short, but she didn't say any of these things because she avoided the fight. Noemi was going to do whatever she wanted, regardless. Unless Ma saw her with her own eyes, she knew Ma wouldn't believe her clothes. Even that posed a problem because Noemi's wardrobe would only cast suspicion on Jasmin's wardrobe. Rock and hard place.

"Ahem," Noemi cleared her throat.

Sea. Jasmin underlined.

"Ahem," Noemi cleared her throat again.

"Ready?" Jasmin asked.

"Yeah," she admitted, "but you aren't."

"Yeah, I am," Jasmin confessed. "I'm not changing. If you can't go with me like this, then I'm not going." Jasmin wore a gray Looney Toons t-shirt, wide legged blue jeans, and black and white Chuck Taylor's. It was what she wore to school almost every day. She was sure no one noticed what she wore at school and was even more certain that they wouldn't notice at the stupid game either. They did their job, covered what needed to be covered, didn't keep her too hot, nor too cold unlike Noemi's confused wardrobe with her extra warm on top sweater and her extra nothing shorts on the bottom. Her poor body didn't even know what temperature to prepare for.

"Calm down, Chica," Noemi rolled her eyes, "you forgot one."

"One what?" Jasmin asked.

"Extremity," Noemi said.

"Huh?"

"Yeah, underline *extremity*," she advised. "Ms. Perez gave us that same poem last year. I see she hasn't changed her assignments."

"Oh," Jasmin said. She hadn't realized that they had the same teachers. Jasmin guessed it might happen, since they were only a year apart. Hesitantly, she underlined the word.

"Good," she approved. "She's probably going to give you the same vocabulary quizzes too. I got the answers to those if you want."

"I don't want," Jasmin declared. What teacher would give the same quizzes year after year without changing the answers? *Stupid,* Jasmin thought. And who would even save these things and for what real reason? Unless she was planning on repeating the same class. But, that didn't make sense either. Jasmin did want the answers. Jasmin wanted things to be easy, easier like they seemed to be for Noemi but she didn't want it that way, not the wrong way. Is that what she did, cheated? Jasmin watched others cheat all the time, never getting caught. She was sure that if she ever even thought about cheating, she'd be the first one in Hobson history to get caught and Ma'd kill her for sure.

NOEMI HELD JASMIN'S hand as they walked towards the school, reminding Jasmin of when she did this without Ma forcing her, before she left Jasmin for her friends, when they were in elementary school, but never in middle school though. By then, Noemi was already becoming Jasmin's not-sister. This, though, felt good, like the past. Jasmin leaned into Noemi briefly resting her head against her arm.

Woah's and *Aww's* seeped out the gym as they trickled in.

"Two, please," Noemi told the lady at the front door who sat at a table with an iron box.

"We have to pay?" Jasmin asked.

"Yes," the lady winked at Jasmin. "But the student's price."

"That's stupid," Jasmin said to no one in particular.

"All funds go to the basketball program here," the lady said as if justifying why the school charged money to kids without jobs.

"We got it," Noemi unfolded a wad of money, removed a bill, then gave it to the lady.

"Where'd you get that?" Jasmin's eyes widened. Ma never gave them actual cash in their hands unless they were going somewhere and as far as she knew, they weren't going anywhere. When Ma did give them money, it most certainly wasn't in the form of the lump that Noemi quickly put back into her pocket. Why hadn't Jasmin noticed this bulge before?

"Get what?" Noemi chuckled.

Jasmin followed her into the gym. She had so many questions. If Ma gave her that money, why didn't she know about it? *There's no way*, Jasmin thought.

Both teams were at opposite ends of the court throwing several balls from one player to the next. The stands filled with all sorts of people, students, parents, even little kids that were in no way old enough to attend high school. Jasmin passed by the gym several times but had no idea that it could hold this many people. Even the stands on the second level were filled. A sea of orange also colored the stands. Immediately, Jasmin understood why Noemi looked the way she did. Jasmin tugged at her clothes feeling a little awkward. Maybe she should've changed, but into what?

"Noemi?" Jasmin called but her voice faded into the eruption of screams and shouts from the stands, Noemi continued on.

All eyes seem to have been on the court when they walked in. One player tossed the ball in the air to another as he jumped to meet it mid-air, catching and slamming it into the basket in one swooping motion. Sometimes a player used one arm to do this and others used both arms. Each time, the crowd erupted with blaring screams, and each time the crowd screamed, Jasmin's entire body cringed. This seemed more a show than a game.

"Come on," Noemi gripped, pulling Jasmin and slightly pushing her in front. "We gotta find a seat before it gets full."

Was she kidding? Jasmin wondered as it was already a packed house. Never had Jasmin seen this many students all in one place, not even at lunch. There was no way they would find a seat amidst this chaos.

"It's full, Noemi," Jasmin pointed out. "We should've come earlier."

"Naw, up there." She pointed to a small spot in the stands. Climbing carefully, they hoped not to fall. With each step, the stands shook.

"We're not staying long, right?" Jasmin asked. She was already feeling the angst of being surrounded by a crowd with no exit. But, Noemi had already joined the mass raising her arms and shouting each time a player dunked the ball. Jasmin had lost her; her gaze was on the court like the rest of the hypnotized crowd.

"Yeah-ya," Noemi screamed, springing from her seat with the others who created a shelter of humans around Jasmin. The player's two feet landed with a thud and the crowd erupted again. With his long dreadlocks in his face, he flexed his lengthy tattooed arms toward the crowd and they erupted again. People stumped their feet on the benches, making the stands shake like Jasmin imagined it would feel during an earthquake. Florida didn't have earthquakes, right?

"Really?" Jasmin rolled her eyes. She may have been the only one in that gym not intrigued with what was happening on the court.

"Chill," Noemi suggested.

"When does the game start?" Jasmin asked. "Better question: When does it end?"

"Ladies and gentlemen, at this time we ask that you please rise and remove your caps as we honor America with the playing of our National Anthem," a deep voice announced.

"This is serious, huh," Jasmin said to Noemi as they joined the standing crowd.

"Shush," Noemi instructed.

Players from both teams, their coaches, and everyone else in the stands stood with arms covering hearts facing the American flag that hung next to the scoreboard. A soft female's voice piped out the lyrics, extending the "*rockets red glare*" without ruining the tune.

"Let's play some basketball," the announcer continued after the recording ended on "*the home of the brave*." "We want to welcome..."

"Seems like it's going to be a long night, Noemi," Jasmin complained. "We should've at least called Ma to let her know we were going to be out. I'm sure she's not going to mind, especially since this is a school activity."

"We'll be back before she's home," Noemi suggested. "Now, for once in your life, chill and do what other kids do."

Now

"Jasmin," the school's resource officer, a slim, tall woman almost taller than Detective Sanchez, called her name like she knew who she was. Her gun belt hung loosely, lower than it looked like it should be. Jasmin wondered how she knew who she was because lots of kids were walking towards them, and she was not someone who anyone knew, especially the school's resource officer.

"Yes," Jasmin stared at them both. Other kids glanced but didn't stop because no one wanted detention for being late.

Detective Sanchez's white shirt was painted onto his body, shoulders erect, muscles begging to be set free. Didn't he know that his shirt was too small? A thin, long orange tie was tightly knotted around his neck, clearly not a clip-on. His dark blue pants were almost as tight as his shirt. Boldly, his gold badge hung on the outside of his belt shouting to everyone that he was not "just a resource officer." All eyes were on them, including the eyes of those in the office. Everyone, including Jasmin, was probably wondering why Detective Sanchez was there.

"Let's go in here." The resource officer opened the door to the office, then followed. Closing the door drowned the sound of feet shuffling and kids shouting in the hallway. It did not however avert staring eyes that wondered what was going on. "Detective Sanchez has some information he needs to share with you."

Jasmin's heart beated loudly like someone violently banging on drums. *Thump. Thump. Thump.* She wondered if anyone else heard it shouting out the hope that she had. Or was it fear? *Why isn't Ma here with him? Is he even allowed to talk to me without a parent?* Jasmin wondered. Every single show she'd watched had a parent present during interviews. But, *this*, Jasmin wondered. *What is it?*

"Ok," she swallowed loudly.

"Just some follow up questions," Detective Sanchez said.

Her heart sank. Hope gained wings and flew away. Just questions, follow up questions. No information about her sister. *Shouldn't you be outside looking for her? Following leads or whatever they say?* But, Jasmin didn't tell him how to do his job.

"You can use my office." The resource officer adjusted her gun belt. Yep, it was too heavy for her. Jasmin imagined her running down the hallway with it. *Will it fall off if she doesn't hold on?*

"I'd like to take a walk," Detective Sanchez announced. "If that's all right."

"Well, we prefer," the resource officer paused. "Yes, that's all right."

Jasmin tightened her grip on her backpack following the detective into the hallway. Although the bell had already rung, a few kids still straggled in the hallway. They stared at them as if seeing a unicorn.

"How have you been?" Detective Sanchez asked like they were old pals who hadn't seen each other in a while.

"Did you find out anything about my sister?" Jasmin jumped right in. *I don't have time to be nice to this man who is yet to find my sister. Tell me something other than asking a stupid question. Of course, I'm not well. Should I say, I'm peachy? Best day of my life, sir.* "Does Ma know you're here?"

"No," he paused. "And yes."

"Yes, you have information about my sister? No, you've not told Ma?" Jasmin placed the words in the order in which she wanted them to be.

"Ms. Hobson knows I'm here, in fact, she suggested it'd be a good idea since Noemi is very much involved in school and has lots of friends, possibly people who may know where she is." He stopped and stared at Jasmin. "Is this true?"

"I guess," Jasmin answered. "Yeah, she does a lot here. People know her," not like they didn't know Jasmin, but she left that out.

"Have you spoken to anyone about her?" He stopped at the glass case that stored trophies, large and small, and framed pictures on several shelves.

"What do you mean?" Jasmin asked, confused. "Like her friends?"

"Yes."

"Was I supposed to do that? Isn't that like," Jasmin swallowed choosing her words wisely, "I mean, what do I ask exactly?"

"It's still there," he leaned closer to the case peering in.

"Huh?" Jasmin said.

"My pic," his lips spread across his face proudly.

"Oh." Disappointed, Jasmin stared at the picture too. It was him, a younger version of Detective Sanchez except, in the school's basketball jersey. Posed with one leg resting on a basketball and a trophy in his hand, he stood tall like a lion perched on a large rock overlooking its pride.

"That year, I was number one in the state for taking charges," he said. "The entire state."

Jasmin didn't know what that meant so she said nothing.

"Tell me some names of some of your sister's friends."

"I don't really know *know* any of them," Jasmin admitted.

"A first name, at least," he pushed. "Anything?"

"She's with the theater people," Jasmin responded. "But I don't know their names." They were usually Romeo, Claudius, or Annie, but as for the names their parents gave them, Jasmin had no idea.

"Ms. Bitters still runs the theater troupe?" he asked.

"Yeah," Jasmin answered.

"I took her class once because I needed easy credit. It's not as easy as it looks," he chuckled.

Why was he even laughing? Wasn't there another way to do this? Shouldn't they be in an office, his cubicle, at the police station looking at possibilities? Posting pictures of Noemi? Shouldn't he be asking Noemi's friends the last time they saw her?

"How is any of this helping Noemi?" Jasmin rubbed her eyes in exasperation hoping he didn't hear her annoyance.

"Does Noemi need help?" He stared at Jasmin.

"Of course, she does," Jasmin blurted out. "Why wouldn't she? She's clearly missing."

"Missing." He rolled the word on his tongue. "Why do you think she's missing?"

"I don't know." Jasmin clenched her fists squeezing her nails into the palm of her hands. *Because she's not here and have been gone for some time now. MISSING!* Jasmin shouted on the inside but instead said, "I just know she's not here at school. She's not at home. But we're here, doing this, whatever this is."

"It's a process, Ms. Hobson."

"A process?" Her eyes welled up to leak something fierce.

"Yes," his voice was low and calm. "Because she is a teenager..."

"A child you mean."

"Yes, a child," he continued. "We are taking every measure to find her. You and your mother did the right thing by coming to the station immediately. There's a misconception that one should wait 24 hours to report a child missing; but I'm glad that you knew what to do so that we could get right on it."

"Ok, but."

He placed his hand on Jasmin's shoulder with a light touch. "Trust me, we're doing everything that we can to find her."

It does not feel like WE, whoever WE is, is doing everything. How can a detective looking for someone, or doing everything, look where we said she isn't? But Jasmin didn't say any of this, instead she wiped the tears from her eyes.

At the wooden double doors which closed off the theater kids from the rest of the world, Detective Sanchez pulled on one making a loud creaking sound but not loud enough to draw attention. In a huge room with rows of seats surrounding a stage, students sat in outfits they probably didn't wear to school. No one usually walked around looking like a bird, not on purpose anyway.

"Again," Ms. Bitters shouted. "This time, with feeling."

"Just like I remember," Detective Sanchez mused.

"Can I help you?" Ms. Bitter's peered at them over her thick rimmed glasses.

"Sorry to interrupt you," he said.

"What do you need?" Ms. Bitters said impatiently. She wore a dress printed with colorful birds, perhaps a costume of some type. Her dress dragged on the floor as she walked towards them.

"Ms. Bitters, I'm Detective Sanchez and..."

"I remember you," she cut him off. "A detective?"

"Yes, I just had some questions."

"Carry on," Ms. Bitters shouted to the class. The kids on the stage continued their performance.

"I'll be quick," Detective Sanchez disclosed. "I wanted to talk to you about one of your students."

"Yes?"

"Noemi Hobson." He removed his cell phone from his pocket.

With her right eyebrow raised she said, "Yes?"

"How was she during your last rehearsal? You are currently practicing for a performance, correct?"

"She wasn't here last night. In fact," she looked at the stage to make sure the students were still practicing lines, "she hasn't been here for a while."

"What's a while?" Detective Sanchez typed on his phone while listening to Ms. Bitters.

"It's been months, actually." She turned to look at the students on the stage. "I've actually had to recast her as Audrey."

This was news to Jasmin because Noemi had been singing these songs throughout the house. Where was she going if not going to rehearsal? Did Ma know?

"*Little Shop of Horrors*, right?" Detective Sanchez said sheepishly. "I was one of the angry plants when I was here."

"Carnivorous," Ms. Bitters corrected him. "Carnivorous plants."

"When was the last time you've seen her?"

"I'm not sure." She stared at the stage again. "I was devastated when she decided to quit theater."

"Quit?" Jasmin gasped. *Is this why Noemi told her she didn't have to wait for her at rehearsals? She'd quit?*

"Yes, quit." Ms. Bitters looked at Jasmin as though she hadn't realized Jasmin had been standing next to Detective Sanchez this entire time. "I tried my best to talk her into staying. She has an amazing voice. In fact, this is why I thought she'd be a perfect Audrey."

"What did she say, exactly, when she decided to quit?" Detective Sanchez asked.

"She said she was overwhelmed and needed a break. I get that. She's been the lead in most of my plays. Sometimes the great ones need a break." She glanced at the stage again. "She'll be back. She's a good one. I had to give *Audrey* to Becky, Noemi's understudy. She's not Noemi, but..."

"You have to have theater as a class to be in theater, correct?" Detective Sanchez asked.

"No, not necessarily. You can be a part without being in the class. Noemi does take this class, though."

"Has she been in class?"

"To be honest, Mr. Sanchez?" she admitted, "you're not on stage, I don't really know if you're here or not."

"Ok, thanks for your time, Ms. Bitters," Detective Sanchez said. "It looks like you're going to have another great production!"

"From the top," Ms. Bitters shouted to the class walking away from Jasmin and Detective Sanchez.

"A dead end," Jasmin sighed.

"Not necessarily," Detective Sanchez corrects her. "We know a lot more than we did prior to this visit."

"We're still no closer to finding Noemi," Jasmin fumed.

"Did you know Noemi quit theater?"

"No," Jasmin answered. She should've known. Several times, she and Stephen had walked Noemi back to school for rehearsals. Yeah, she'd get a ride home because most of her friends drove their own cars. If not rehearsals, where was she going?

Detective Sanchez returned Jasmin to the front office where the office clerk promptly wrote her a pass for her next class. She walked to her class with even more questions than she had before.

This detective is no help, she concluded. *Me and Ma are going to have to find Noemi ourselves.*

Then

Jasmin tried to *chill* as Noemi suggested but it was very hard, as hard as the bench they sat on. She'd never sat on anything so stiff. Not even the cafeteria seats were this hard. Unlike Jasmin, Noemi didn't fidget much in her seat. Plus, she was out of it many times, like the rest of the crowd. People shouted and screamed every time the Lions scored. There couldn't have been anyone from the opponent's team in the crowd. If so, they stayed quiet.

"You want something to eat?" Noemi asked Jasmin over the loud cheers.

"No, thank you," Jasmin screamed.

"I'm going to get something." She eyed the door they'd walked through earlier. "Be right back."

As she sauntered towards the entrance, she stopped several times to say hello to someone, hugging and continuing on her way. Eventually, she disappeared through the door behind the throngs. Weren't they a fire hazard to blocking the door like that? Everyone seemed to be hypnotized by what was happening on the court. A few seconds left on the clock and the Lion's star player had the ball in his hand. He ran down the court spacing himself from everyone else. They knew they weren't going to catch him. He slammed the ball into the basket at the same time the buzzer erupted. Everyone jumped and screamed. The stands exploded in the now familiar earthquake-like fashion. The teams ran off the court and into the locker rooms. Now only half time; they had the other half of the game to go.

Noemi still hadn't returned from concessions when the dancers rushed onto the court, each one more "perfect" than the other. As if they were clones, they were perfectly synchronized. Though they wore different colored body suits, each of their heads were styled in the same fashion, a neat ponytail at the top. Each face showed bright paint, not quite clown-like, but not quite movie star either.

Where was Noemi? She missed probably the most important part of the game, the dancing. Jasmin wouldn't admit to Noemi, but this was probably the most entertaining thing about the game. She continued to watch as each girl moved deliberately. They all knew their moves and when to move. Had that been Jasmin, she would've probably stomped on everyone's toes, leaving them bloodily toeless and the school without a dance group for half time.

The players streamed back onto the court. With half time over, the Lions now led. The crowd still screamed and hollered each time the Lions scored. There was little time left on the clock, no way that they could lose. The time had come for them to leave so that they could beat the crowd before everyone stampeded out of the gym; however, Noemi still hadn't returned. Her seat, next to Jasmin, stayed hard and empty. The line to the concession couldn't be that long, could it?

Worried, Jasmin carefully picked her way down the stands and onto the side of the court. Falling in front of the entire school was the last thing that she wanted to do. Each time the referees and players ran in her direction, she stopped, waited, then continued towards the door. Still the mob stood as if they were not blocking the entrance and now technically, the exit.

Two people stood in line at the concession stand which was right outside of the blocked entrance, neither of whom was Noemi. The aroma of freshly popped popcorn wafted from the concession area. Maybe Jasmin did want something after all, but focused on Noemi's whereabouts, she ignored the scent to look around. Except for these two at concessions and the lady who collected the money from the nonworking students, and Jasmin, there was no one else. Jasmin didn't panic, though. She had to be somewhere around here, right?

"Where's the bathroom?" Jasmin asked the lady.

"Down the hall, hon," she pointed to the empty hallway.

Two bodies tightly hugged into one were plastered on the wall. Neither made a move as Jasmin passed by them.

"Noemi?" Jasmin peeked her head into the girls' bathroom. "You in here?"

At the mirror, a girl in an oversized sweatshirt from which shorts peeked out, painted dark red lipstick onto her salmon colored lips. Jasmin glanced under each stall, opening the doors of the empty ones. None revealed Noemi. Lipstick girl looked at her, her thin eyebrows furrowed.

"You seen a girl in here?" Jasmin asked. "Big sweater, short shorts?"

"Naw," she shook her head.

She looked to be about Jasmin's age but she wasn't someone she remembered from her classes. *Great, asked a girl in the girl's bathroom if she saw a girl. That was some dope detective work.* Where was Noemi?

"Thanks," Jasmin said and returned to the game.

People still stood and cheered. Weren't they tired? She'd lost her seat, so she sat on the very first row with her arms between her legs. Surrounded by a cacophony of oohs and aahs filling the gym, she waited. People shouted. She waited some more. Her eyes searched the gym looking for anyone who looked like Noemi, any indication that she was still here. Nothing.

The game ended with the Lions in an overwhelming victory. Everyone seemed excited but Jasmin and the losing team. They hung their heads as they tapped the hands of the players from the Lion's den. What a crazy ritual, not a word between players. People streamed out of the gym. The game was over and Noemi still hadn't returned from concessions.

EXCEPT FOR JASMIN AND the janitor, only a few stragglers remained among the wrappers and crushed soda cans. Why were people so nasty? The janitor, a portly woman, probably way older than Ma, meandered up and down the stands, picking up the trash and placing it into a large, black plastic bag. At her pace, she'd never finish before school the next day. Voices floated from the locker room. Basketball players emerged two by two, each pair joshing with the other, excited. No one noticed Jasmin. If they did, they didn't say anything.

"You gahtu to go," the janitor snuck up on Jasmin, speaking in a heavy island accent.

"I can't," Jasmin admitted. "I have to wait for my sister."

"Well, you cyan wait in ya," she said continuing to pick up the trash.

Jasmin left, not wanting to be told a second time to leave. It was strange that she was the only one who sat as though waiting for the players when, in fact, she waited for her sister who'd said she'd be "right back." Jasmin believed her again, that she really wanted to spend some time with her, do sisterly stuff like she said. But, as before, Jasmin fell for her charm, her manipulation. She'd hoped this time to be different but no. She hadn't changed one bit in bringing Jasmin along under false pretenses. Jasmin had "fun" until she disappeared. No, it wasn't fun watching a game she cared nothing for, listening to strangers scream insanely. But she was with Noemi, her big sister, so no matter. *This was going to be us: me and her doing us.* Never again though. Noemi would never leave her again!

A full moon floated boldly in the skies, illuminated by a few lamps so that her shadow joined her body as she sat on the stairway. Stephen would've been perfect company. No doubt, he would've tried to convince her to walk home by now, but she couldn't go home, not without Noemi. What about Ma? What was she going to tell her? Jasmin imagined the conversation.

Jasmin as she walked through the door: *Good night Ma!*

Ma: *Where's your sister?*

Jasmin: I don't know

Ma: You don't know?

Jasmin: She was with me, then she wasn't.

Ma: GO GET HER and DON'T COME HOME WITHOUT HER. What did I tell you about separating?

Jasmin imagined Ma yelling at her because Ma didn't want them ever separated. She also thought of the possibility of this, getting home without Noemi, ending up being her fault. Dutifully, Jasmin attended rehearsals and Noemi's other activities, so that they would never be apart. *Safer together*, Ma said. Noemi didn't follow that rule, though, leaving Jasmin each opportunity she got.

Jasmin wondered if Noemi even thought about her when she left her alone. She couldn't possibly.

That's it, Jasmin thought. *I'm gonna tell Ma. Got to.* This was getting out of hand, leaving Jasmin alone. Where was Noemi disappearing to? This had to be some sort of safety issue. *It'd be for her own good*, Jasmin mused, *telling Ma. For her safety. But if I tell Ma, that means we're never leaving the house again.* The possibility of never seeing a movie again because of Noemi's behavior clouded Jasmin's decision. Although Jasmin didn't care about going to another basketball game, she cared about her movies. It was the one thing she enjoyed and telling Ma could jeopardize that.

Jasmin heard the BOOM! BOOM! of the car before she saw it, its dark windows shielding the passengers. She looked away so that it didn't seem as though she was trying to peer into someone's vehicle. But, how could anyone hear themselves in a car so loud? The sound annoyingly increased inching closer. A black car with shiny rims stopped directly in front of her, the separation, the lower stairs.

"Come on," Noemi yelled out the window, music blared. "We're getting a ride home."

"Naw," Jasmin looked away. "I'm good."

Who knew where she had been? Or this driver? Jasmin was not climbing into a strange person's car. That was not how she was going to end her life. Noemi hadn't even apologized for leaving her there. No explanation. A ride home wasn't going to make up for it. They didn't live far enough from the school for her to bribe Jasmin with a ride home. Jasmin gathered herself and started walking. At least, now, Jasmin knew where she was and that she was safe. Noemi? Worried about Jasmin? Never.

Now

Stephen kicked a stray rock along the sidewalk that led home from school. They both walked with other students leaving school. Some were going home and some to friends' houses. Jasmin would never even think about going to Stephen's house. Not ever. Even though Ma allowed him to visit theirs, that was not something the girls were ever permitted to do, go to other people's homes. Cars impatiently honked their horns to hurry the meandering kids in the crosswalk. However, the hoard of students continued to walk without purpose or urgency.

Jasmin thought about when Ma began to tell them about why she didn't want them going to other people's homes. They were at the kitchen table when Noemi randomly asked, "Ma, why don't you like us to go to nobody's house, I mean, you don't want nobody over here either."

Ma gazed off into the distance like she was thinking about something else before she answered, "I can't see in other people's houses. I don't know who's there."

"But Ma," Noemi protested. "What could possibly happen? Parents are there. Other kids our age."

"How do you know?" Jasmin interjected. Noemi sounded as though she'd been in other people's houses although Ma told them not to.

"I'm just guessing," Noemi rolled her eyes at Jasmin.

"Noemi and Jasmin," Ma looked at both girls intently. "Lots could happen. Lots."

"Like what?" Noemi pressed.

"I never told you girls this," Ma paused.

Both Jasmin and Noemi leaned in as though Ma was getting ready to share some deep dark secret.

"When I was younger," Ma swallowed as though thinking about the best way to share what she wanted to share with her girls. "Just trust me, some pretty houses are not as pretty inside."

"What does that even mean," Noemi complained.

"It means I don't want you going to other people's houses and I don't want anyone in here," Ma stated as though she'd given the correct answer instead of creating more questions in their minds.

"Zero point seven three, three, three percent," Stephen broke the silence.

"What's that?" Jasmin asked.

"It's the number of people found each year." Stephen pushed the rock along, determined to take it as far as he could.

"Why would you say that?" Jasmin blurted out. Her face tightened as she stared at Stephen. "Noemi is not one of your statistics."

"She's not, but," Stephen softened his voice.

"But, nothing," annoyance slithered from her. As much as she loved Stephen, this was not one of the times she needed to hear his, his blind "optimism."

"It's hope, Jaz."

"Hope?" she spat. "You're serious right now?"

"Yes, Jasmin," Stephen kicked the rock again. "It means there's a chance of finding her."

"First off," Jasmin angrily swallowed. "Noemi's not missing, she's..."

Jasmin didn't finish the words because the truth was that she was missing. She didn't know if she was just off on one of her *trips*, but she felt that, like many other times, her sister was going to appear in her self-absorbed state: unapologetic, and everything was going to be "all right." Noemi was going to show up, late, like always. Jasmin was going to be angry at her as usual. Most importantly, Jasmin was going to forgive her like she normally did. These thoughts filled Jasmin's mind, forcing out the raw and unnerving statistics that Stephen chose to comfort her.

"Jaz," Stephen called. Time and distance colored her thoughts. She was surprised that they were in front of her driveway so quickly. At least, their walk seemed faster than usual to her. "It will be ok."

"Sure," Jasmin mumbled. Her legs heavily guided her towards her house leaving Stephen outside with his less than one percent of hope.

Jasmin opened the living room door to see Uncle Dee stretched his entire six-foot-plus frame on the living room couch. *Ma must not be home*, Jasmin thought. His legs were so long that they dangled over the arm of the couch. The living room T.V. was on but no one was watching. Yep, it was going to be hot again, the weather man stated. A disheveled Ma slouched at the kitchen counter, something she always told the girls not to do. Shoulders bolted upright and back a little was the correct stance. Neck perched so that eyes were always looking ahead and not down. *There's nothing down there for us*, Ma always told her girls.

But today, she was not wearing Beyonce nor Tina, but left bald spots on her head exposed. Jasmin couldn't ever remember having seen her mother without her wigs. If so, she certainly didn't recall her thinning hair. *Will her hair look like Ma's at that age?* Jasmin wondered. *Bald in some spots?* Jasmin raked her hand through her hair, worried both about her hair and about her mother's reactions.

"Ma?" Jasmin called. She wanted to tell her that the detective saw her at school but hesitated as he'd said that she already knew. Jasmin tried to think about what to say to her mother, as she grieved at the kitchen table. Had she been there all day?

"What?" Ma answered curtly.

This was not the voice that Jasmin was used to but she continued, "Did you eat?"

The sink was empty and the stove unused. When Ma was home, this was never the case. When Ma was home, the girls knew that they were coming home to a feast, Noemi's favorite, mac and cheese, or to Jasmin's, sweet potato lasagna, a meal that made no sense to Jasmin but found comforting, Ma always made sure they ate home cooked meals when she could. Not today, though. No pot had been touched yet.

"Not really hungry, Jaz," Ma answered, her voice shallow and weak as a dog's whistle.

The dark circles around her eyes seemed to have grown whilst Jasmin was at school. The lines on Ma's forehead now more prominent and dominant, made Ma look older than she did just a few hours ago before Jasmin left for school. Jasmin didn't point that out. *No one needs to tell a frog it's ugly.* Jasmin remembered this saying from her mother as she tried not to stare at a completely different mother, a stranger to her.

"You gotta eat something, Ma," Jasmin said as she shuffled through the kitchen, opening cupboards, removing pans, food from the refrigerator, and placing them on the stove. Even though it was afternoon, breakfast food was the only thing that Jasmin thought was quick enough to save her mother from starvation.

Bacon danced around to its own orchestrated music. Sizzling and popping continued until Jasmin removed each slice, placing each on a plate with a double folded piece of paper towel to soak up the oil. Then, she cracked the eggs on the brim of the frying pan, something Ma always told her not to do because doing that heightened the chances of egg shells getting into the cooked egg. Jasmin looked over her shoulder to see if Ma was watching her. She wasn't. Safe, Jasmin then scrambled the egg in the left-over bacon grease, an experiment she once tried, liked, and was now her specialty. She then added a dash of shredded cheese using the spatula to make sure that the eggs were indeed scrambled. She proudly placed some pieces of bacon next to chunks of eggs, sitting them side by side, kind of like sisters, like how she and Noemi should be. Arrogantly, she placed the well-dressed plate in front of Ma. *She's gotta eat this,* Jasmin thought. *I put my foot in it.*

"I said I'm not hungry, Jaz." Ma violently pushed the plate away from her and it made a crackling sound against the counter top tossing the eggs and bacon around on the plate.

"Ma," Jasmin pled. "You haven't eaten all day."

"I said, I. Am. Not. Hungry," spacing each word so that Jasmin really understood her intent. How could she not be hungry after not eating all day? This wasn't like Ma at all: She was always telling the girls to make sure to eat before school, eat during school, and, eat after school. Fuel is important, she'd say. But this was disobeying her own rules.

"Hmmm," Uncle Dee chomped on the discarded bacon as if it were his. His grinning mouth opened, showing the food inside. "You put your foot in this, girl." One by one, he shoveled the bacon into his mouth. Then, he finished off the eggs leaving the fork and plate clean as if unused. Jasmin shook her head in disbelief. Why was he even there?

It's not for you, Jasmin thought. She didn't ever say what she was thinking, for fear of hurting feelings. She'd rather not make others feel the way they made her feel.

"Jasmin," Ma said, lifting her head.

"Yes, Ma," Jasmin answered.

"You don't know nothing?" Ma stared at Jasmin desperately. "Nothing at all? You see her talking to anybody? During rehearsals? Track practice, anything?"

Jasmin thought for a moment. She thought about telling Ma that Noemi hadn't been to rehearsals for some time, in fact, she'd quit. But, that would reveal that she hadn't been going to rehearsals like Ma told her to. That'd mean that she hadn't been obeying Ma. She was certain that the detective was going to tell Ma and she'd deal with it then. But, for now, she didn't know how and if she could handle telling Ma all that had really been happening.

"No, Ma," Jasmin swallowed.

"I can't believe this is happening to us," Ma sighed, her voice heavy with grief. "To my little girl. Who would even do something like this?"

"I don't know, Ma," Jasmin answered. "I don't know."

"Those things are open to anybody right?" Ma continued. This was the most she'd said to Jasmin since *it* had happened.

"What things?" Jasmin asked.

"Rehearsals and practice," Ma explained. "Anyone could just go and watch right? Did you see anybody then?"

"No, Ma." Jasmin answered.

"Were you even looking, paying attention like I taught you?"

"Yes, Ma. For sure, there wasn't nobody that wasn't supposed to be there," Jasmin heard herself lie. "Nobody except me and sometimes Stephen."

"Ok," Ma submitted, hanging her head.

I should've told her, Jasmin thought. *I should've told her that Noemi didn't go where she said she's going. She always left me and didn't come back til late. But it was too late. Ma's gonna blame me for everything just because I didn't call her the first time it happened. All this was my fault*, Jasmin thought. So, she kept her mouth shut.

Ding! Ding! The doorbell rang and in unison, everyone looked up.

"You expecting somebody?" Uncle Dee asked Ma.

Ma shook her head no.

"You?" Uncle Dee looked at Jasmin.

Jasmin shook her head no. Uncle Dee walked to the door with Jasmin right behind. *Why does he even think that he could answer our door as if he lives here*, Jasmin thought.

Uncle Dee opened the door to see Detective Shawn Sanchez standing with his knuckles perched ready to knock. He was with a short, portly woman. Jasmin noticed who was older than he. His supervisor maybe? Her pants suit was neatly pressed, straight creases in the pants, and with a button down collared shirt. No tie unlike Detective Sanchez who sported the same outfit Jasmin saw him in earlier. Jasmin didn't remember ever seeing her, but she never forgot a face, not really anyway, not important faces.

"Sir," Detective Sanchez said. "I'm Detective Sanchez and this is my partner, Sergeant Murdock."

A sergeant? Jasmin thought. *Why are they here? Why didn't they both come to school?* Many questions clouded Jasmin's mind; then she stopped breathing for a moment. *Oh god. Is this happening?*

On her T.V. shows, every single one of them, the only time two cops went to a front door was to give bad news. She looked at Ma, still slouching at the kitchen counter, then at Uncle Dee who seemed to be clueless. Jasmin knew how all this worked. She knew that two cops only came to the door to tell the family that their loved ones were... dead.

Sweet Potato Lasagna - Jasmin's comfort food

Ask Ma for permission to use her ingredients and stuff.

Ingredients

2 or 3 medium to large sweet potatoes

1 can of crushed pineapples

cinnamon/brown sugar

Peel and slice the sweet potatoes. Drain the crushed pineapples or the lasagna will be soggy. Layer a smallish (not cupcake small) pan with the sweet potatoes and the crushed pineapple. Make as many layers as the ingredients will allow. Sprinkle with a little cinnamon or brown sugar or both if you like. Bake at 400 degrees for about 40 minutes or until potatoes are soft enough.

Then

Like a predator scoping out its prey, the car crept behind Jasmin who still refused to ride with a total stranger. This was something Ma always told the girls not to do, get in a car with strangers. Now, Noemi's gone and done that, the very thing Ma told her not to do. Roping Jasmin into disobeying wasn't going to be easy for Noemi.

"Come on, Jaz." Noemi rolled down the window's pane and sang out, "I don't want you on these streets alone, girl."

Now she was worried? Jasmin thought. Where was she when she was supposed to be sitting next to Jasmin, when they were supposed to be having a sisterly time. Jasmin remembered her saying that she was going to college soon, so they really needed to spend that time together. *How were we going to spend time together, when you're always leaving me alone*? Jasmin rolled her eyes feeling gullible and disappointed in herself for allowing Noemi to beguile her once more. *Was it wrong to keep hoping that she would act better*? One thing Jaz knew though, she was not riding in that stranger's car.

"You know you're being ridiculous, right?" Noemi asked, not expecting an answer. She knew how headstrong Jasmin could be. If she said she wasn't going to do something, she very rarely did change her mind. In fact, Noemi couldn't ever remember a time when Jasmin changed her decision and it vexed her, vexed her in such a way that she shouted, "Jasmin. Ophelia. Hobson. Get in this damn car!"

"Oh, we're swearing now?" Jasmin whipped her head around in shock. "Why don't you tell the world my social security number too?"

Noemi knew that Jasmin didn't like hearing swear words, just as much as she didn't use them. But, she mostly knew that she particularly didn't like her middle name. "You don't want me to call you that, then get in the car and let's go."

Jasmin continued her trek, now adamant about not accepting the ride, not only because she didn't know the driver but, mostly because she couldn't believe that Noemi had left her yet again. Her return didn't come with an apology. It never did. This was not something that Jasmin could ever get used to. She almost wished that Noemi would leave for college already, so she'd be alone. She was tired of being ignored. Lied to. Bamboozled? She laughed at that word, bamboozled. Was this even a *bamboozled* situation, Jasmin wondered, trying to keep her mind off the black car, with dark tint, that her sister now hung her head from, slowly following her. This was definitely a scene out of one of her cop shows. Detective Benson would tell her to run, look for a safe place, preferably with lots of lights or lots of people or lots of lights and people. But this wasn't the situation. This wasn't that. This was her vainglorious sister, not caring for anyone but herself.

"You really are something else," Noemi accused.

"Me?" Jasmin placed her palm on her chest, more vexed than annoyed. *Was she serious right now?* "YOU can't be serious."

"It don't take all of this, Jaz," Noemi pleaded, both arms hanging out the car.

If Ma saw her, not only would she be angered at her for being in a stranger's car but she'd be angry and disappointed that she hung out of the car like some addict. Jasmin almost wished Ma could see how Noemi behaved except she'd get in trouble too. Jasmin thought about that. Maybe she could get in the car so that they'd be home quickly, preferably before Ma, and they wouldn't have to explain where they'd been. Jasmin wouldn't have to explain that she'd been waiting while Noemi was God-knows-where. What if this car pulled off just when Ma rode up? What if Ma saw them in the car? Then what?

So she wouldn't waste more time trying to figure out Ma's whereabouts, Jasmin stopped suddenly and pulled on the passenger side's door.

"I thought you wanted me in," Jasmin sneered. "The door's locked."

"Try it again," Noemi smiled. She got exactly what she wanted and loved it.

Jasmin pulled on the door a second time and it opened easily. She sighed loudly and climbed in. *Leather seats?* Soft seats and a clean car? Not like Ma's who had a bunch of work stuff in hers and just enough room for her and Noemi and once in a while, Uncle Dee. A mix of peppermint and lemon permeated the air. Jasmin was slightly dazzled; however, the fascination quickly disappeared when the loud music returned to the car. *Who could even hear in this thing?*

Except for the bit of light from the dashboard, the rest of the car was dark. Jasmin peered in the rear-view mirror hoping to catch a glance of the driver. Nothing. All she could see was the fold of the hoodie on his neck. *Ok*, she thought, *Broad shoulders, too, but I ain't never seen him.* Jasmin reminded herself that she didn't know half the people that Noemi knew, so it was quite possible that the driver did go to school with them.

Noemi reached over and lowered the volume, easing the pressure off Jasmin's ears.

Good, Jasmin thought because she didn't want to end up with a hearing aid at such a young age.

"Pull over here," Noemi commanded.

"I can take you all the way home," the deep voice said. He didn't sound familiar and Jasmin took note of that.

"Naw, we're good right here," Noemi explained. "Pull over right here." She directed the driver to pull over on the side of the street. At the sidewalk, the girls still weren't right in front of their home.

What was the point of getting in the car? Jasmin wondered. *All that time wasted coaxing me in just so we could get out a few yards later?*

They were just a few streets away from their home, close enough to get there in a few minutes, but far enough so that if Ma was home, she wouldn't see who or what brought the girls home. Jasmin saw what Noemi was doing. She saw her plan. If Ma was home, she could tell her whatever story she wanted to. But, if Ma saw the car, that'd be a whole other mess she'd have to clean up.

Noemi opened the door allowing lights to flood into the car, "Thanks." She stared back at Jasmin as though silently telling her to say the same.

Jasmin was not going to say *thanks* or anything else for that matter. She had already gotten into a car with a totally faceless person and that was all Noemi was going to get out of her. Plus, she was still bitter from having to sit on those hard seats in the gym without Noemi.

Noemi ignored Jasmin's blatant disrespect and extended her face over to the driver's. Their lips joined together and lingered as though both of Jasmin's eyes weren't there to witness. *How rude*, Jasmin thought. She thought about the kids making out in the hallways at school as though no one else could see. She wanted to shout "*get a room*" but didn't from fear of what Noemi would do.

"Ugh," Jasmin grunted, but that only prompted Noemi to put her hand up to the man's face, a face that Jasmin realized was covered in hair. The lights revealed thick, long, black dreadlocks neatly tucked into a ponytail. *That's what the hoodie hid*. His portrait didn't give Jasmin enough information to identify him. She knew, though, he couldn't have been anyone she'd noticed in school. *Would I?* Jasmin thought. *Who was this bearded guy?* He didn't have patches like Jasmin knew most of the boys in school had. From what she saw, he looked like a grown man, too grown for Noemi.

Jasmin exited the car making her way towards the house. She was not going to stare at Noemi and her... whatever he was. The less she saw, the better.

"Wait up, Jaz," Noemi called out. She jogged to her side. "You're walking too fast."

"Am I though?" Jasmin stopped, staring at her as though looking for her to say something, anything, anything that would explain what happened. Why did she feel the need to lie to her? Make her wait? Disappear? Anything. Anything that showed she had some sort of respect for her sister. *Forget the respect*. Jasmin thought. *Love. Do you even love me?* But Jasmin said none of this.

"Yeah, Jaz," Noemi maintained. "You could've waited."

"Waited?" Jasmin gasped. "For what?"

"For me, silly," Noemi playfully hit her on her shoulder. "Plus, you didn't even say hi to my friend."

Jasmin continued walking home. Although they weren't far, it was still a school night and still late. "He's not my friend."

"He won't be if you continue to be this rude."

"Good!"

"You know, he's actually a really nice guy," Noemi explained.

"Good!"

"He's going to take us to the Homecoming parade," Noemi continued.

"Wonderful!" Jasmin said sarcastically. "Wonderful."

"Don't be like that."

Jasmin marched towards home, passing similar houses on their way. It's a good thing that their neighbors weren't nosy. If so, they'd be concerned about why they walked on the streets so late. Noemi followed closely and tried to walk lockstep with Jasmin. Each time she caught up, Jasmin quickened her pace. She had no intention of talking to Noemi. There was nothing she could say that could explain what she'd done. As they turned the corner, Jasmin spied Ma's car as it sat in the driveway, having apparently been there for some time.

"Great," Jasmin complained. "Ma's home."

Now

"**M**ay we come in?" Detective Sanchez asked. He looked at Uncle Dee questionably, remembering that Mrs., No, Ms. Hobson had said about no man being in the house. He made a mental note of this but stuck to the task at hand.

"What for," Uncle Dee launched defensively, "we got rights!"

"Uncle Dee," Jasmin pacified a clearly agitated Uncle Dee. "This is the detective who's helping us find Noemi. He's here to help, right?" Jasmin looked at the detective hopefully, although she knew what was coming. She knew this was what two cops did: one notified and the other consoled.

Jasmin wondered if Ma was going to be the dramatic type, the type that would slap the detective upon hearing the bad news. Or was she going to do it? *Am I strong enough?* Jasmin wondered. *Certainly not tall enough.* After all, they hadn't done a very good job of finding Noemi, in her opinion.

"Yes," Detective Sanchez confirmed. "Yes, we are."

"See?" Jasmin said to Uncle Dee but still braced herself. "They're here to help."

"My partner and I," Detective Sanchez looked at his partner. "We just have some follow up questions."

Jasmin released a loud breath, relieved for the questions rather than the notification. As much as she was sometimes annoyed by her sister, her death wasn't something she was ready to hear. And Ma, how was she going to deal with that? Deal with Noemi being...

145

Jasmin swallowed loudly hoping no one else could hear her harrowing thoughts.

"Let them in," Ma shouted from the kitchen.

Uncle Dee reluctantly stepped aside making sure to keep his eyes on their every move. Ma finally pushed up from the kitchen's island where Jasmin was certain she'd spent the entire day to join them.

"Any news?" Ma begged. "Anything?" Her eyes bulged from her head now, red and watery.

"No," Detective Sanchez said. "Not yet."

"Then, why are you here?" Ma yelled. "You should be out looking."

"Yeah, why you ain't out there putting up stickers or something?" Uncle Dee chimed in.

"Ms. Hobson," Sergeant Murdock ignored Uncle Dee. "We wanted to confirm some things with you."

"Like what?" Ma asked. "I gave this one here, everything at the police station. Her picture, date of birth, everything you need to find her."

"Yes, and we thank you for that," Sergeant Murdock lightly touched Ma's arm. "Is there some place we can sit?"

"Yes," Ma guided her to the large couch, taking Uncle Dee's blanket and tossing it behind the couch where it landed on the floor.

"We want," Sergeant Murdock sat next to Ma. With Detective Sanchez on the other side of Ma, she continued, "we would like to ask some more questions."

"I answered a lot of questions downtown," Ma spat. "Tell me what you've done to find my daughter. Why don't you have any kind of news to give me? I know they say that no news is good news, but I need to hear something, know something."

"I know, Ms. Hobson," the sergeant lightly placed her palm on Ma's leg. "This cannot be easy."

"You got children?" Ma asked.

The sergeant paused and looked down at her legs, "No, ma'am."

"Then don't tell me what it can and cannot be, cause clearly you don't know."

"Ms. Hobson," the sergeant ignored Ma's demeanor. She's seen this before and chalked it up to a concerned parent "Tell us about Noemi's boyfriend."

Suddenly a loud crashing noise streamed from the kitchen as though a bunch of plates had fallen to their deaths. Everyone immediately looked up to see what had happened but the question still lingered in the air.

"Ms. Hobson?" Sergeant continued, ignoring the possible mess in the kitchen. "Noemi's boyfriend?"

"Noemi doesn't have a boyfriend," Ma declared. "You must be mixing her up with someone else. The girls aren't permitted to date."

Both the detective and the sergeant looked at each other when Ma said this. Jasmin switched from one leg to the other. As far she knew, Noemi didn't have a boyfriend, per se. At least no one she knew, no information she could give them.

"Ok," the sergeant persisted. "Does Noemi have any male friends, any one that you can think of?"

"No," Ma was certain of this but then she looked at Jasmin. "It's just my two girls."

Jasmin shook her head, agreeing with her mother but left her eyes on the ground hoping to disappear. *Maybe not a boyfriend, per se,* she thought, *but there are people. Boys, no, men.* She didn't say anything though, but kept her mouth shut and switched her leg again.

"I mean," Ma said as though she was just remembering something important. "There's Stephen and that's it. They all three hang out together. Is that what you mean?"

"Yes," the sergeant pulled out her phone and began to type, "tell me about Stephen."

Ma glared at the phone. "You don't have paper or something?"

"Excuse me?" the Sergeant asked.

"It's ok, it's ok," Ma repeated to herself. "Stephen goes to school with the girls. He has for years, right Jaz?"

"Ok," the sergeant nodded her head and continued to type in her phone. "Is Stephen Noemi's boyfriend?"

"Noemi does not have a boyfriend," Ma persisted. "I said this already."

"All routine questions, Ms. Hobson," Detective Sanchez added.

"NO. Stephen is the girls' friend. Tell them Jaz," Ma dragged Jasmin into the conversation.

He's really my friend, Jasmin wanted to say. Instead she submitted, "Yeah."

"See?" Ma snapped, "The boy lives down the street. He's always here. We know where he is. What we don't know is where my child is. I thought you were here to help."

"We are, Ms. Hobson," the Sergeant said. "We're just covering all our bases, trying to get all the answers we can so that we can locate your daughter."

"You're the girls' father?" Detective Sanchez directed this question to Uncle Dee as he rejoined them in the living room.

"No," Ma cried. "I told you their father died. This is my brother, their uncle."

The Sergeant typed something on her cell phone.

"What you typing over there?" Uncle Dee asked suspiciously.

"When was the last time you saw Noemi?" Detective Shawn asked Uncle Dee but noted his uneasiness, his unwillingness to cooperate.

"He's barely here," Ma answered. "He doesn't see the girls often, not often enough anyway."

Jasmin wondered if this was something that Ma truly wanted, Uncle Dee seeing them more often. It was definitely not something she'd expressed in the past, but she seemed to want it now. Or was this the Ma that was thinking irrationally because she was looking for Noemi?

The Sergeant typed something again on her phone.

"You're doing it again," Uncle Dee tightened his jaws and accused. "What are you typing?"

"Mr...." The Sergeant stopped and realized that she didn't have his name. "What is your name?"

"That's not important," Uncle Dee mumbled and left for the kitchen.

"Deonte James," Ma added, ignoring Uncle Dee. "If you think it'll help."

The Sergeant patted Ma's clasped hands and assured, "It will."

"But he's rarely ever here, when he is," Ma paused, "you know?"

"Yes," the sergeant replied. "Thank you for clearing that up."

But what did Ma really clear up? Nothing. While Uncle Dee was barely there, he was still family and they had to check all the leads, right? Jasmin thought about the questions they asked about Stephen and how they were now on to Uncle Dee. She understood the need for the questions but felt as though time would be better served outside, out there, somewhere, where Noemi was.

"We would like to look around Noemi's room," the sergeant said, releasing Ma's hands. "Can you show me where it is?"

"You got a warrant?" Uncle Dee exclaimed.

"Dee, please," Ma said tiredly then pointed to the stairs. "It's just up the stairs there. Jaz, take them please."

Jasmin led the sergeant up the stairs leaving Ma with Detective Sanchez and Uncle Dee back in the kitchen pacing back and forth like he was about to run a marathon. The door creaked as Jasmin opened it. *It's never done that before,* Jasmin thought, *at least I don't think so.* Pillows askew on the bed just like Noemi didn't like. She bent down to fix them, so that when Noemi came back, it would be as she'd left it.

"Is her room usually so neat?" The sergeant looked around.

"Yes, ma'am," Jasmin said, remembering to make Ma proud in her responses to adults.

Plastered on the walls were large canvases of Noemi, mostly of her on different stages in her various plays. Her face was as perfect as Ms. America's, blemishes not to be seen, unlike Jasmin's cumbersome freckles. She wondered sometimes if they were even related.

"She's pretty," the sergeant noted. It was the general consensus that everyone arrived at when they saw Noemi because, she was. The sergeant settled on the largest canvas. Noemi's thick, black curly hair peeked from a dull yellow bandanna tied at the back of her head. Her sleeveless but collared shirt was knotted at her navel, just where the waist of her denim bell bottom pants began. She stood tall as one lightly muscled arm hung free and the other held a phone receiver up to her ear.

"Where was this taken?" the sergeant asked.

"At school."

"Hmm," the sergeant mused. "It's pretty mature for her, no?"

"She's Beneatha Younger here," Jasmin added.

"Ok," the sergeant sounded unsure.

"From the play, *A Raisin in the Sun*," Jasmin remembered. While Noemi was usually excited about almost all the musicals in her theater group, this play was the one she most talked about. She worked day in and day out practicing her part, rehearsing her accent, forcing Jasmin to run lines with her. Jasmin didn't mind as much because it meant time together, but then it got fatiguing because Noemi just had to get it right.

"'That's the character that dated two different men, right?" the sergeant asked. "The young girl in college?"

"The one who wanted to become a doctor," Jasmin corrected.

The Sergeant moved over to the closet doors and gasped when she opened them. Hosts of stuffed animals spilled on the carpet as though they were only being contained by the closed door. Most, the girls won from the fair on the rare occasions Ma took them. Some, though, didn't look familiar to Jasmin, like the large plush rabbit with the red heart sewn on its chest.

That's new. Jasmin thought. Robotically, Jasmin began to gather the stuffed animals, the turtle, the rabbit, and others.

The sergeant began to help, "This is a lot. You must have many in your room, too."

"I don't," Jasmin admitted. Unlike Noemi, she was not athletic so when it was time to knock those bottles down with a baseball or make a basket three times in a row to win a stuffed animal, Jasmin always failed.

"What's this?" The sergeant pointed at a red backpack that looked like it was trying to stay hidden.

"Her school bag," Jasmin lied. Both the girls' backpacks were the same, black Jansport. This was new to Jasmin and she wondered what else Noemi had hidden in her closet.

Then

"Where've you been?" Ma opened the door just as Noemi put her hand on the doorknob to enter. She had her car keys in her hand and her small bag draped across her body.

"At school," Noemi lied. "Ma, you missed it."

"Missed what?" Ma asked. "And why were you at school this late?"

"Ma, you had to be there," Noemi ignored Ma's main question.

Ma looked at her watch waiting for an answer from the girls.

"You gonna let us in?" Noemi asked.

Ma stepped aside following Noemi into the kitchen. Jasmin followed behind, vowing to stay quiet. She had no idea what Noemi was up to and quite frankly didn't want to be a part of it.

"It's almost midnight," Ma paused, hanging her keys back on the key rack. "What could you have been doing at school at this God-forsaken hour?"

"Well," Noemi said calmly, "if you let me, I'll tell you."

"The only thing open this late is..." Ma stopped herself.

"I thought Jasmin and I should start spending some time together." Noemi opened the refrigerator's door and closed it back, not finding what she was looking for. "You know? Like you always say."

"Yeah, good idea, but it's still way past the time you're supposed to be in the house. Way past." Ma put the kettle on. If this was going to take some time, she was going to take this opportunity to have some tea with her girls. Though late, the ritual was still something she cherished.

"I know, Ma," Noemi admitted. "But, we had to. Plus did you know that Jasmin has never been to a basketball game?"

"No, I didn't know that," Ma confessed. "I didn't think she'd be interested."

I'm not. Jasmin thought. *And tonight didn't change that.*

"Well, I took it upon myself," Noemi hung her arm around Jasmin. "To take Lil' Sis to her first basketball game."

It took every ounce of patience Jasmin had left not to shove Noemi's arm from around her; but, she let it stay and played along.

Ma looked at both of the girls approvingly. While it was ridiculously late for the girls to have been out of the house, this is what she wanted, for them to be close, getting along, hanging out together, like sisters should.

"But still so late," Ma muttered.

"We were at the school though, one of the biggest games of the season," Noemi's excitement filled the room. "Right, Jaz?"

How would I know? Jasmin wanted to say but instead, she shook her head yes.

"So many people were in the stands, too, we could barely find a seat."

"You could've put it on the calendar," Ma suggested. "Give me a heads up. Ask permission even."

"Ma, honestly," Noemi removed the whistling kettle from the stove.

"I'll do it," Ma offered. She removed three mugs from the top cupboards and three chamomile tea bags from the pantry. It was too late to drink anything else.

"I didn't really even think about it until we got home from school," Noemi continued. "For real."

"Ok, but next time, I want you to," Ma looked at both girls intensely over the brim of her mug. "I need to know where you are. When you'll be home. Why are you going? The usual. This doesn't tell me why you were out this late, and on a school night."

"I'm 'bout to tell you," Noemi carefully sipped her tea.

"I am about to tell you," Ma corrected.

"Yeah, that," Noemi said, ignoring Ma's correction. She knew she was supposed to start over and repeat what Ma said but she didn't. "They were shooting threes after threes. Each time the other team scored, our school would answer back with their own three pointer. Ma, they kept doing that all night."

Jasmin's insides burned, but not from the scalding tea.

"Half time came," Noemi sipped again. "You really should let me join the cheerleading squad because those girls CAN NOT dance."

"No," Ma declared. "You've got too much going on as it is."

"True," Noemi shook her head. "Did you know half time is like twenty minutes to like ten days?"

"What?" Ma asked.

"It was the longest half time ever. So long that it felt like ten days," Noemi lied.

"I've never been interested in those things," Ma stated.

"After half time, our guys came out fired up, ready to go. There wasn't a missed basket. The crowd went wild. Ma, I mean wiiilld."

"Still late though, no?" Ma persisted. "I can't believe a game goes so late. I was about to head up there."

"Ma," Noemi rolled her eyes. "It's not that serious."

"It is," Ma answered. "When you're out this late."

"Anyway," Noemi continued. "The other team started coming back, chipping away at the score. Ma it was so close. I thought for sure we had it. You know? We were going to win without a problem."

Jasmin wished she'd remember how it really went but she was focused on Noemi's story. *Who was this girl*, Jasmin wondered. She lied so easily to Ma, like it was second nature.

"Did they win?" Ma asked excitingly.

"Well," Noemi dramatized, her voice one of an actress who knew her craft. "You'd think it was that easy, right, cause our team is really good."

Jasmin looked at the time on the stove. They were up way past their bedtime, and they still had school in the morning. She wanted Noemi to wrap up her tale quickly, but she kept adding more and more to her story.

"They're top in the county," Noemi added. "But the other school is top in their county too, so imagine."

"Since when do you know so much about basketball?" Jasmin asked. She'd regretted the moment the words left her mouth because she swore not to get involved.

"Since when do I not know everything?" Noemi scoffed at Jasmin. "Anyway, Ma, they chipped away at the lead that we had until it was a two point game; we led by two points. With one second left in the game, a guy from the other team, number two I think, Jaz, was it number two?"

"I don't remember," Jasmin answered curtly.

"Jasmin," Ma moved closer to Jasmin, tucking one of her braids behind her ear. "You didn't have fun?"

"Yeah, she did," Noemi answered. "She was screaming with the rest of us when it happened because those two points meant that we were in overtime. I don't even know how they had all that energy, Ma."

"So that wasn't the end of the game?" Ma leaned in, fascinated.

"No, Ma," Noemi admitted. "They put five minutes on the clock and basically started over the game. We won the tip off though."

"Good," Ma said as though she really understood.

"But the same thing happened again. Both teams wanted to win so badly that they went into another over time, and then another. Ma, I thought it was never going to end until one of our guys made a shot from half court."

"Half court?" Ma said dubiously. "Isn't that a long shot?"

"Literally, Ma." Noemi confirmed. "He won the game for us, though, and kept us from going into a quadruple overtime. Man, Ma, we probably wouldn't have made it home until morning if they'd kept going like that. But it was a good game, right, Jaz?"

Jasmin shook her head in agreement. Unlike Noemi, she didn't lie. It was a good game. It just wasn't a good game for her.

"Well, I'm glad you had a good time," Ma exclaimed.

"We did," Noemi confirmed.

"I'm especially glad you spent some time together. Come here." Both girls moved towards Ma. With each of Ma's arms draped over her girls, she pulled them into either side of her body and hugged them tightly. She kissed both on their foreheads and said, "Good night girls, you still have school in the morning."

"Yeah," Noemi said. "Is there any way we can skip?"

"Nope," Ma said. "This is the price of supporting your school. Glad your team won though!"

Both girls left Ma in the kitchen and headed up the stairs to their respective bedrooms.

"Thanks for the help back there," Noemi whispered sarcastically. "You've really got a sister's back."

Now

"Why would she leave her school bag?" the sergeant mused. "Didn't she take it to school with her?"

Jasmin shrugged her shoulders, an action she knew Ma hated, especially when speaking with adults.

"When was the last time you saw your sister, again?" the sergeant searched Jasmin's face.

"I don't know," Jasmin answered. The room began to shrink around them. "I told the cop downstairs this information al-"

"Detective Sanchez?" the Sergeant interrupted. "Yes, he told me but, this," she held the bag upright as though she could see through it with some sort of special cop X-ray eyes. "This shouldn't be here, should it?"

"We walked to school in the morning, just like we normally do," Jasmin explained.

"And she didn't take her backpack?"

"Yeah, she did," Jasmin thought back. "Why wouldn't she?"

"Just questions, Jasmin," the sergeant said, detecting an edge in Jasmin's voice.

"She left us, just like she normally does," Jasmin allowed her mind to take her back for a moment. She and Stephen were walking to school as usual with Noemi in front with her normal crew. She had her backpack but it was definitely not red. It was not what the sergeant was holding. Ma bought the girls the same backpack for as long as Jasmin could remember, same color, same size. They didn't get a new one every year either, only when it broke and it rarely did. So, this, this red thing with a small monkey hanging from the zipper, where did it come from?

"Us?" The sergeant broke into her thoughts.

"Me and Stephen."

"So, is Stephen here a lot? Was he here when Noemi disappeared?"

"No," Jasmin blurted out. "I mean, yeah,"

"Which is it?" The Sergeant placed the bag on Noemi's bed.

Jasmin looked at the bag, the bag she'd never seen in her life. *Whose was it and why was it even there?*

"Which is it?" The sergeant repeated, her voice just a little bit louder than before.

"Yeah, Stephen's here a lot," Jasmin clarified. "But that's Stephen. He's been walking to school with us since we were little." *This was not about Stephen,* Jasmin wanted to say but didn't.

"Where's Stephen now?"

"I don't know," Jasmin said defensively. "Probably home like everybody else except Noemi."

The Sergeant took a mental note of Jasmin's curtness and agitation when she asked about Stephen. She opened the red backpack and the sound of the zipper opening filled the room like a cat squealing.

Jasmin quickly grabbed the bag, yanking it out of the detective's hand, "Don't you need a warrant for that?"

The sergeant eyed Jasmin suspiciously, "These are exigent circumstances, Jasmin."

Exigent? Jasmin thought. *That's when the cops burst through people's doors because they hear a noise inside or something. But, Noemi was not even here. This was what they should be doing at someone else's house.* At least this was what she saw on T.V. This woman, the sergeant, was not like Detective Shawn who Jasmin felt was a much better help than the Sergeant. Maybe it was his age, much closer to the girls than this stout woman who seemed to want to search through Noemi's stuff rather than actually search for her. She kept asking about Stephen when he had nothing to do with Noemi's disappearance. *Disappearance? Was this what this was? Was Noemi not coming back?* Jasmin tried to shake the negative thoughts from her mind.

"It's probably just her school stuff in there," Jasmin offered. "Books and stuff."

"We're only here to help, Jasmin," the Sergeant softly closed her hand over Jasmin's and slowly removed the bag from her tight grip. "We want to look at this from every angle."

Like rain unsure if it should fall, tears trickled one by one, each taking their time to roll down Jasmin's face. This was more real than T.V. where they found the missing person within an hour. Noemi's been gone longer than that. It was more real than some news report, where Ma prayed they would find the missing girl alive. This was happening now. She was in the middle of a real-life *"missing person's case?" Disappearance?* She didn't want to be a *Hulu* special so she prayed silently that Noemi would burst through the door for Ma's punishment and they'd go on with their lives. This, what was happening, was not who they were. They were not "cops-in-your-house-people," not in the least bit.

A cell phone, a notebook, a pair of shoes, and several articles of clothing fell out of the backpack and onto Noemi's bed as the sergeant turned the bag upside down.

"Interesting," the sergeant picked up the cellphone. "These things are usually glued to teenagers."

"It's not hers," Jasmin admitted.

"Then, whose is it?" The sergeant flipped it over in her hand then back again to its face.

"We don't have phones."

"You don't?" the sergeant asked suspiciously.

"Neither of us do," Jasmin continued. "I mean, Ma has one but just for work."

"How do you keep in touch with your mother, then?"

Jasmin lowered her head, "I guess we don't."

"Interesting," the sergeant mused. She then touched the small screen but nothing happened. Then she pressed the side of the phone with her finger and a white apple lit up in the center of the screen. Four, round circles sat at the top with instructions to enter the passcode.

"Do you know the passcode?" The Sergeant looked at Jasmin.

Jasmin shook her head, no.

"Would your mother have it?"

She shook her head faster this time, no, again. Definitely not.

"We'll have our lab techs look at it." The sergeant put the cell phone aside to pick up the notebook. She flipped through it, not reading, but looking through it as though she could read from the sides of the pages. Lines were scribbled in the book but neither read the words.

This could be a good thing, though, right? Jasmin thought about the ways the T.V. shows she watched used cell phones to track people's whereabouts. *Could they use this to find her last known location? Maybe? LAST. KNOWN.* This sounded all too surreal for Jasmin, too out of the ordinary. *This was not us,* she reminded herself. *I've got to focus.*

"This is wet," Jasmin picked up a piece of clothing, blue jeans, the short ones she'd seen Noemi wear but knew Ma didn't buy.

"Damp," the sergeant corrected. She took it from Jasmin holding it out in front of her, then she lifted it, taking a quick whiff and quickly pushed it away. "It smells."

"If it's wet," Jasmin began.

"Damp," the sergeant interjected. "Interesting."

"Damp," Jasmin repeated, not caring about the difference. "Doesn't that mean that it was just placed here. That she couldn't have been gone for long?"

"It could," the sergeant mused. "When's the last time you said you saw your sister, again?"

"The same time I told Detective Sanchez," Jasmin quipped. Time was getting away from them and she saw no need for the repeated questions especially since they weren't producing viable answers.

"Interesting," the sergeant mused.

"What's interesting about that?" Jasmin yelled. "Where's Noemi? You're here searching through her stuff instead of looking for her. She's clearly not in that bag."

The sergeant stayed silent.

Jasmin flailed her arms. "Where is she? She's not in her room. Not in the house. Not here at all." Tears flowed like a relentless downpour, rushing and cascading down like a torrential rainstorm.

"Jasmin?" The sergeant called, "Jasmin, listen to me."

"You don't understand." Jasmin whimpered.

She stepped closer to Jasmin closing the gap between them, "What don't I understand?"

"You don't get it," Jasmin exclaimed. "None of you do."

"Tell me," the sergeant urged. "We are only here to help."

"This is not Noemi," Jasmin waved her arm at the bed. "All this."

"All what?" The sergeant urged again.

"This," Jasmin confirmed. "She would never not come back. Never."

Then

"Let's go somewhere!" Noemi excitedly suggested as she walked up the stairs towards Jasmin. Jasmin thought for sure she was going to tell her to get off the computer, but she didn't.

Jasmin clickety clacked away at the keys searching for anything that could help pass the time. She had completed all her homework and sat idled. On school holidays, it was usually hard to pass time, especially when Ma wasn't home.

"Like where?" Jasmin submitted. There wasn't anything they could really do. All of Noemi's friends were at the beach, where the cool people go on a school holiday. Noemi couldn't go to the beach, though, because of Ma. If Ma's not there, then it's not safe. Jasmin's friends, well, Stephen, he was at home, most likely playing video games.

"I don't know," Noemi stood behind Jasmin slowly rubbing her shoulders. "We could just walk to the mall and hang out."

"I don't think so," Jasmin shook her shoulders so that Noemi's hands fell away. They didn't. "The last time *we* went to the mall, *I* was the only one there."

"That was one time, Jaz," Noemi's voice softened. "That'd never happen again Jazzy poo."

"Jazzy poo?" Jasmin said suspiciously, "Now I know you're really up to something."

"We can't just stay cooped up in this house all day." She threw herself down on the small couch next to the computer.

"I'm fine with it," Jasmin said dryly.

"Girl, you're going to die in this house," Noemi warned.

"I'm fine with that too," Jasmin looked around and nodded with approval. "There are worse places to die, so this is fine."

"Girrrrll," Noemi begged. "Come on, you've been glued to that seat since you got up. Ain't nothing in that little box that's more interesting than outside."

Jasmin thought that Noemi was probably right, but she hadn't had a great track record with her companionship. She was still suspicious.

"But," Jasmin paused, "we didn't ask Ma if we could go."

"But we didn't ask Ma if we could go," Noemi mocked. "We'll be back before she's even home."

"I don't know, Noemi," Jasmin answered reluctantly. "You know how she behaves when we're not where she expects us."

"Come on, Jazzy poo," Noemi whined.

"Come on, nothing."

"Let's just go! We ain't doing nothing here." Noemi continued to plead her case.

She was right. They weren't doing a thing. Jasmin had read as much on the Internet as she could and couldn't read anymore. The same stories were starting to come up again, begging her to read them again.

"You sure we gonna be back before Ma?" Jasmin asked.

"Promise," Noemi jumped off the couch.

"You know we could just call her and ask before we go, just to make sure, right?"

"You know she'll say NO and we'll end up right here, doing nothing as usual, right?" Noemi was back behind Jasmin, rubbing her shoulders again, carefully massaging them so that Jasmin could feel at ease.

"Ok, stop," Jasmin yelled, "you're gonna break my shoulders."

Noemi stopped, a large grin filling her face, reflecting on the computer screen. "Yeah, Jaz!" she screamed.

SWEAT DRIPPED DOWN both the girls' faces as they journeyed towards the mall. That was at least one of the perks that they had, living in their neighborhood, nothing too far. School was close, mall nearby, everything a stone's throw's distance. Regardless of proximity, the sun reigned and forced the girls to wish they had walked with a towel to wipe their damp faces, the sweat from their armpits, and their necks. Sweat seeped from every part of their bodies.

As soon as they arrived at the mall, the girls headed directly to the second floor, the food court, where they knew that they'd be able to cool off. Jasmin crashed at one of the round tables next to the railing, one that allowed them to look down at people on the first floor. Noemi headed straight to Chik-Fila because she knew she was more likely able to get a cup from them than from any other restaurant in the food court.

"May I get two cups of water, please?" Noemi asked the cashier in her nicest voice.

The lady handed her two plastic cups, not the ones that they served regular drinks in, but smaller, clear plastic ones without their logos. "It's my pleasure," the lady smiled.

Noemi filled both cups with water from the soda fountain and made her way back to Jasmin.

"Thanks." Jasmin gulped the water hoping to put out the small fire in her throat. She reminded herself that to do this again, with the sun only two miles away from earth, she would definitely walk with a towel and a faucet or her own personal air conditioning unit.

"Dang, girl," Noemi said in shock. "Thirsty much?"

"Just a little," Jasmin laughed.

"Here," Noemi handed her cup to Jasmin, "have mine."

Jasmin gulped that one too. Noemi returned to the fountain with both empties while Jasmin fiddled with her shoe lace under the table. Those things always seem to rattle themselves free any time they felt. Jasmin looked up in search of Noemi. She should've been back already as the table was near the counter.

What the? Jasmin asked herself. Noemi wasn't getting the water like she said nor was she next to the soda fountain. Her eyes darted around the food court, slowing at the lady handing out chicken samples. She made a mental note to eat those later. *Where'd she gone so quickly*, Jasmin wondered. It was happening again. Instead of actually being and spending time together like Noemi said they would, she had vanished. Jasmin was so sick and tired of Noemi's selfish behavior, but what could she do? *Not fall for it again*, Jasmin vowed. *Never again*. A small part of her began to worry how long this new stint would last. Long or short? The whole day? She hadn't even brought money to entertain herself at the movies. Either way, this time for sure, Jasmin vowed to leave the mall with or without Noemi. She was not going to wait like she'd done before.

"Jaz," Noemi startled Jasmin. "This is Bakari!"

Jasmin focused on the red hoodie and matching red sweat pants revealing the waistband of his underwear. *Wasn't he burning up in that thing*? she wondered. Large, wireless headphones hung around his neck, too large for his ears for sure. His hair was just as long as Noemi's but instead of a ponytail like Noemi's, he wore a big and proud afro. His eyes were gray which Jasmin thought were colored contacts since the color was unnatural. *Already a lie*, she thought.

"So?" Jasmin said coldly.

"Don't mind my sister," Noemi looked at her friend. "She's not released from her cage often."

"I'm ready to go home," Jasmin whined. "There's nothing here to do, and I can do nothing at home."

"Bakari and I are going to walk around the mall some," Noemi ignored Jasmin's whining. "I'm not going back home. Not right now, anyway."

"Noemi," Jasmin pulled her aside and whispered. "Really, though? You're doing this? We don't even know him."

"How are you going to know him without even trying?" Noemi announced, ignoring Jasmin's intent to have a conversation with her sister.

"Noemi," Jasmin pouted. "Let's just go home. Please. Ma's going to be so mad at us."

People busied themselves around them. Some even stopped for the samples that Jasmin still hadn't gotten.

"Don't be a child, Jasmin," Noemi suggested. "If you wanna go home, go."

"You coming?" Bakari asked Noemi impatiently.

"Yeah," Noemi answered.

"Noemi?" Jasmin pleaded. "We gotta get home before Ma gets back."

"Go Jasmin," Noemi spat. "No one's stopping you."

Noemi hooked her arm in Bakari's and walked off leaving Jasmin to decide whether to hang with them or return home. She wanted to go home, back to her safe, stranger-free home. But, Noemi kept walking.

Though Noemi was just a bit shorter than he, from behind they looked like a perfect couple, the kind that had been together a long time. Jasmin trailed behind, silently hoping the outing was over soon. She was going to be back home, and back home before Ma. *Never again*, she thought. *Never again.*

Now

Only the sounds of Jasmin's sobs filled the room. With this new.... evidence, Jasmin thought, *what did all this mean? Where was Noemi?* Jasmin's palms began to sweat and her chest began to tighten as though the air attempting to leave her lungs was trapped. She tried to calm herself: *One. Two. One. Two,* but her chest felt heavier each time she tried to release the air ensnared in her chest.

"Breathe," the Sergeant gripped both of Jasmin's arms. "Breathe with me." The Sergeant sucked in a deep breath and held it for a second then let it out. "Like this."

One. Two. One. Two. Jasmin counted and inhaled as deeply as she could. Though shallow, the breaths left her body as they should.

"That's it," the Sergeant encouraged. "That's it."

One. Two. One. Two. The breaths became deeper and deeper as Jasmin continued to practice the breathing. She collapsed on Noemi's bed next to the phone and the damp clothes, relieved to breathe freely again.

"Thank you," Jasmin said to the Sergeant, "I mean, really."

"You're welcome, Jasmin," the Sergeant answered "You said something earlier that I wanted to address. Are you up for some more questions?"

Not really, Jasmin thought but answered, "I am. Anything."

"You said," the Sergeant studied Jasmin's face intently. "You said that *she'd never not come back.* What did you mean by that?"

Jasmin rubbed both her palms on her thighs, carefully thinking about her answer, "What do you mean?"

"Look," the Sergeant stressed. "Clearly you know more than you're telling us. You spend more time with your sister than anyone in this house so we're going to need you to be honest. Now, what did you mean by that? Has Noemi done this before? Gone somewhere without you or even your mother knowing?"

"Yes," Jasmin admitted.

"How often has she done this?"

"Not often," Jasmin swallowed. Her chest was threatening to tighten up again, but she inhaled and exhaled, deeply and slowly.

"Give me an estimate," the Sergeant pleaded, "once? Twice? How many?"

Jasmin covered her face with her palms, "Noemi will kill me if I say anything."

"She could be in danger right now," the Sergeant urged. "Anything you can tell us will be helpful. Anything. You want to find your sister, right?"

"Yeah," Jasmin paused. "I mean, yes. I do."

"Where did she go?" the Sergeant asked, "and with who?"

Jasmin wished she knew the answers. She thought about times that Noemi left her and returned as though nothing had happened. Every time, she swore not to go out with her again, but that didn't last. Jasmin squeezed her eyes shut trying to form images in her mind, trying to remember if she'd actually seen anyone with Noemi. Maybe she could describe them to a sketch artist for a picture. She tried to think of a partial license's plate or anything that could help find Noemi but, in actuality, she'd never paid attention. On the many occasions Noemi had gone and left her, she just reappeared like Houdini escaping a trap.

"I don't know," Jasmin shook her head. "I don't know where she could've gone."

"Ok," the sergeant resigned.

"I really don't know anything," Jasmin assured her.

"If you think of anything else," the sergeant pulled out a card handing it to Jasmin, "anything at all, call me."

Jasmin flipped the card in her palms a few times and then pushed it into her pocket, "Sure."

Jasmin watched as the sergeant shoved the damp clothes back into the red backpack but kept the cell phone in her hand.

"You're taking that?" Jasmin asked.

"Yeah," the sergeant casually threw the bag over her shoulder. "This could be a clue to your sister's location."

WORDS FLOATED UP THE stairs as Jasmin and the Sergeant returned to the living room.

"How often are you here, sir?" Detective Shawn asked Uncle Dee.

"Since I've been here," Uncle Dee dragged the back of his palm across his face, wiping off leftover food. "You ain't ask no questions that'll help find my niece. You want to know all this stuff 'bout me but nothing 'bout Noemi. Really, though?"

"He's right," Ma sat on the couch where the Sergeant and Jasmin left her. "How's this going to find my daughter?"

"This what they do, Grace," Uncle Dee spat. "They come looking into your stuff to turn stuff around on you instead of actually helping you. This don't make no kinda' sense."

"Sir," the Sergeant interjected. "We use routine questions to eliminate possible suspects."

"So, I'm a suspect now?" The muscles in Uncle Dee's jaws tightened as he paced back and forth. "See what I mean, Grace?"

Ma used her fingers to smooth out the wrinkles that were definitely mounting on her forehead, "Dee, just answer the questions."

"I'm not doing this," Uncle Dee yelled. "I'm outta here." He stormed out of the house slamming the door behind him.

Both the detective and the sergeant looked at each other.

"Ms. Hobson," the sergeant sat next to Ma. "We know these are uncomfortable questions but they must be asked. Do you understand?"

Ma shook her head, "I know."

"What's Noemi's relationship like with her uncle?" The Sergeant asked.

"What do you mean?" Ma asked.

"Are they close?" The Sergeant continued.

"No," Ma answered. "Not really."

"They don't spend any time together?" Detective Shawn interjected. "No time at all?"

"Barely," Ma straightened her body. "Look, I know what you're getting at. Dee doesn't have anything to do with this. Nothing at all."

"Just covering all the bases," Detective Shawn added.

"He would never." Ma shook her head agreeing with herself. "He would never."

"I think we have all that we need for now, though," the sergeant handed an identical card to Ma, one like she'd given to Jasmin.

Ma examined it then shoved it into her pocket.

"But, if you think of anything else, please reach out to me or my partner. Anything at all," The Sergeant added.

"What's the next move?" Jasmin asked. "What do we do now?"

"Usually," the sergeant answered, "you wait. We do the groundwork. Shawn's been at the school but we'll return because we have some follow up questions."

"What's the chance of Noemi being found?" Jasmin asked, knowing that the odds weren't really in her favor but still hoping.

"Jasmin!" Ma yelled. "Why would you even..."

"Ma," Jasmin pointed out. "She's been gone over two days now. She hasn't called or nothing. If you don't find them in the first twenty-four hours..."

"This is not one of your T.V. shows, Jasmin. She's coming back." Ma cried. "She is."

Ma's right. This was not one of Jasmin's T.V. shows. If so, they would've found Noemi at least within an hour of her disappearance, before the show was over.

Then

"Noemi!" Jasmin yelled. "Wait up." What could she do at this point? Go home? If so, she'd be worried about Noemi the entire time that she was home. Not enough web surfing could wash that worry away. Plus, what if Ma was home? How would she explain that to Ma? What would she say?

"Glad you came to your senses," Noemi looked back and said.

Like a puppy, Jasmin followed the two through the mall watching as Bakari comfortably intertwined his fingers with her sister's as though they were used to being together. *Were they?* Jasmin wondered. She watched as Noemi giggled at everything that Bakari said, even words that didn't make sense. She watched as the two gazed at matching shoes and matching outfits in the store windows. Was she going to get an outfit too? Were they going to be walking around the mall like triplets?

"Jaz," Noemi interrupted her thoughts. "We 'bout to head out."

"What do you mean head out?" Jasmin stared at Noemi suspiciously.

"Us," Noemi twirled her finger around to indicate all of them.

"Yo, you got a twelve in these?" Bakari walked away with a guy who wore a black and white striped shirt.

"Noemi, I want to go home," Jasmin tugged on Noemi. "We don't even know him."

"Bakari?" Noemi asked. "He's cool."

Jasmin stared at Bakari who sat on one of the wooden benches with several boxes of shoes stacked nearby. "I have never seen him in my life. Does he even go to our school?"

"Naw," Noemi smiled. "At least not anymore."

"Ready?" Bakari asked, hands empty of boxes and bags.

"We're not going anywhere with you." Jasmin stepped between the two with her back towards Noemi. As tall as he was, her short legs wouldn't allow her to meet face to face with him.

"Lil' Sis buggin'," He laughed and headed towards the exit. "Yo, you coming or not?"

"Not," Jasmin answered for both of them. "Noemi, let's go. Ma would not like this. Not at all."

"Relax, Jaz," Noemi coaxed. "Sometimes you just need to relax. We're not doing anything people like us don't do."

"People like us?" Jasmin asked, confused.

"Yeah, teenagers," Noemi hooked her arm in Jasmin's and led her to the door where Bakari waited impatiently.

"We do just fine, Nome. I don't want to go. This doesn't even seem right. We 'bout to get into a whole lot of trouble."

"How?" Noemi asked. They walked by store after store slowly, not stopping at any of the kiosks in the center even though they were prompted several times by the salespeople offering free samples. Lack of money made them ignore their knickknacks even if they tried and liked their samples. "We're not even doing nothing wrong."

"We are though," Jasmin reasoned. "What if we go with this guy and we don't get back in time? What if we go with this guy and something happens to us? What if we go with this guy and..."

"What if we go and we have the best time of our lives?" Noemi interrupted.

Jasmin thought about that for a moment. What if she did go and did have fun? What were the odds, though, of her going where she wasn't supposed to go and Ma not finding out? This wasn't something she wanted to do. She just knew that she wasn't going to be able to enjoy herself knowing that they were disobeying Ma.

"No," Jasmin shook her head. "I'm not going."

"Ok," Noemi unhooked her arm from Jasmin's to call her bluff. "See you later then."

Jasmin watched as Noemi caught up with Bakari again to interlace her fingers with his. She stayed close and thought, really thought, about her options. Caught between a rock and a hard place, she had to figure something out and do so quickly. If she went home with Ma there, she'd have to explain where Noemi was and why she wasn't with her. She was not good at coming up with something off the top of her head like Noemi did. She wasn't a good liar. However, if she went with Noemi, she knew if Ma were home when they returned, Noemi would explain their absence away like she had in the past. Jasmin rolled her eyes and quickened her steps intent to catch up with them. In the mall's parking lot, Bakari and Noemi stopped at a two door, silver Civic lodged between a van with no windows and a huge monster truck with wheels that sat higher than the Civic.

"We're going in that?" Jasmin gasped. "Where am I supposed to fit?"

"I got you, Lil' Sis," Bakari declared. He opened the passenger side of the two-door car and pulled the seat forward.

"No," Jasmin shook her head. "I don't think so."

"Really?" Noemi sighed. "This is what we are doing?"

Several people passed by with their shopping bags and glanced at the kids but kept on walking.

"Yo," someone in a car yelled. "Are you coming out?"

"In a minute," Bakari answered him. "What we doing?" He then asked Noemi, "She coming or naw?"

Noemi stared at Jasmin with laser beam eyes, "Get in the car, Jaz."

Jasmin reluctantly maneuvered herself into the car to sit on the back seat. Her stout legs came in handy because they were able to fit tightly like pickles in a jar once Noemi put the front seat back in its place.

"It smells like smoke back here," Jasmin complained.

"Glad your senses work," Noemi said sarcastically.

"It's dreadful, Nome," Jasmin said. "That's a bad sign."

"Stop it," Noemi looked back and said. "Grow up. I could've left you at home but I brought you. You're welcome."

Jasmin sat back in the seat and sulked. She didn't relax. She couldn't. Not because they were in a strange car with a strange man. Not because the music was loud and she couldn't hear herself think. Not because she couldn't really see where they were going so she could identify landmarks. Not because they drove through a neighborhood that looked really sketchy. Not because each time the car met a speed bump, Bakari had to drive around it rather than over it because his car was so low. None of that mattered. All that mattered to Jasmin was getting home and getting home before Ma got there.

Bakari stopped the car in front of a house that looked like all the others. *How'd he know which one was his*, Jasmin wondered. Each looked like a green monopoly house lined up next to each other, but instead of green, they were all a dull peachy color, almost tan with a bright red door. Bakari turned off the car and killed the music at the same time.

"Nome," Jasmin pressed her chin into the back of Noemi's seat and whispered. "This doesn't look right."

Noemi opened the door, pulled her seat back and ignored her complaints.

"Nome, I can't breathe," Jasmin held her palm up to her chest and continued. Her chest felt like an elephant sat on it and at any moment would completely crush her.

"Stop it," Noemi spat. "Don't do this, not right now."

"But," Jasmin complained. "I can't."

"If you can complain," Noemi paused, "then you can breathe."

Jasmin tried to control her breathing the way she's been taught to since she started experiencing breathing difficulties, ever since she could remember. *One. Two.* She began to count in her head. *One. Two.* She did not have a good feeling about the entire situation but would've felt worse had she let Noemi go alone.

Bakari left the car parked next to the curb. Jasmin followed them both up the steps and to the red door that she guessed was Bakari's. A small garden gnome stood in the corner, his jaunty red hat with white dots to one side: with his white, long, full beard, he could've been a little Santa Claus except for his green long sleeve shirt and blue pants. As far as Jasmin knew, Santa didn't wear anything but red.

"You casa, me casa," Bakari said, interrupting Jasmin's thoughts as he opened the door.

That's not even the saying, Jasmin wanted to say but instead she followed her sister and this strange man with the loud, low car into an even stranger house, some place she knew neither one of them belonged. Some place she knew Ma would definitely not approve of.

Now

"Come in," Jasmin beckoned, opening the door before Stephen's knuckles could even graze it.

"How'd you know I was out here?" Stephen asked Jasmin suspiciously. "Are you psychic or something?"

"I wish," Jasmin rushed him into the house. She went directly to the kitchen to pick up her mother's fanny pack from the kitchen counter and wrapped it around her waist.

"Really?" Stephen asked. "I thought you hated that thing."

"I do," she told Stephen. "But this is all I'll need for today."

"That's all you're taking to school?" Stephen asked.

Her fanny pack, well, Ma's, could never fit all the things Jasmin needed for school, certainly not her fat binder that her English teacher insisted that they carry.

"I'm not going to school today, Stephen," Jasmin said, stuffing an apple wrapped in cellophane into the fanny pack. "You want one?"

"No, I'm good," Stephen said, "plenty of them at school."

"I'm not going," Jasmin reminded him. "I've got to figure this thing out."

"Figure what out?"

"I gotta find Noemi," Jasmin said and headed towards the door.

Stephen followed her, "You gotta leave that stuff up to the cops, Jaz."

"It's been days," her words were rapid, leaving one by one like little runners. "They still haven't said anything to us. Nothing. Nothing at all. You know what the odds are after 24 hours, right? Are they even doing anything? We don't know because they're not saying anything, anything at all."

Stephen did the math in his head but was reminded of the last time he gave Jasmin the reality, which she did not like. Instead, he nodded.

"You got your phone, right?" Jasmin asked, knowing that he always did. It was what he played his games on when he wasn't playing on his computer.

"Of course, but..." Stephen said, confused.

"Fully charged?"

"Yeah, but..."

"Ok, let's go," Jasmin rushed through the door, only locking the bottom lock. What else was there to lose after this? Ma was at work as though routines were unchanged. Something about still needing to pay bills, something like that. When she left though, she left each time with puffy eyes and uncontrollable weeping. Jasmin often wondered how she made it through the day because Jasmin couldn't concentrate in school at all. She constantly wondered if Noemi had run away or if she had been taken. If she had run away, why would she? She only had one more year left before college. None of it made any sense to Jasmin.

"Do you even have a plan?" Stephen's voice interrupted Jasmin's thoughts. "You can't just go out there like Dick Stacey asking questions to just anyone."

"Dick Stacey?" Jasmin questioned.

"Yeah, you know? The famous detective, Dick Tracy" Stephen explained. "But, you're a girl, so Dick Stacey."

"Sure," Jasmin answered disinterestedly. "But, that's not what I'm doing," Jasmin explained, as she marched down the sidewalk. If she walked fast enough, she could catch the bus. With certainty, she pulled out the bus schedule to stare at it. "If you're coming, we've gotta get to the bus stop before the bus comes."

"Go where?" Wanting to catch up to Jasmin, Stephen quickened his step. "You're not making any sense."

"Look," Jasmin stopped mid stride to say deliberately, "You don't have to come." What was this strange feeling in her gut? Was it courage? Bravery? Curiosity? She wished she'd had it before. She wished she'd stood up to Noemi and just said NO, forcing them to stay at home where it was safe. So that Noemi would've never been taken? Ran away?

Stephen swallowed. There was no way he was letting her go off without him and then he said with a serious face, "There's no way I'm letting you go wherever it is you're going without me."

"Ok, then." Jasmin quickened her step almost to a jog when she spotted the large, brightly colored bus moseying on down the street. "Let's go."

The bus stopped at the tiny hut just as they arrived. Jasmin watched as the other passengers boarded and paid, some sliding a card in the machine that was right next to the driver and others pushing money into it. Jasmin followed suit, pushing two single dollars into the machine.

"It's for the two of us," she said to the bus driver, but the driver paid her no attention.

The bus was standing room only. Not able to reach the rod in the roof that was meant to be held on to, she wrapped her fingers around the railing of the top of a seat instead. The bus jerked forward and Stephen, who was able to hold on to the roof's railing, gave Jasmin a questioning look.

I hope you know what you're doing, he mouthed.

You didn't have to come, she mouthed back. Secretly, she was glad for his companionship, because while she thought she had an idea where she was going, she wasn't a hundred percent certain. She did know that she had to at least try. Every single passenger, even the ones holding and trying not to fall, were eyes deep in a phone. She couldn't help but wonder if Ma had given them phones if they'd be able to find Noemi, maybe track her location. Call her. Something. Jasmin shoved those thoughts out of her head to stare out the windows as the bus passed businesses, then houses, then houses, then businesses. When the bus stopped at the railroad crossing, the memory of the low driving car inching to get over the railroad tracks filled her mind. *We're getting close*, she thought. *It's gotta be somewhere around here.*

"Next stop is ours," she told Stephen.

He nodded his head.

Before she could tell Stephen to pull the drawstring so that the driver would stop at the next stop, another passenger pulled it and tried to maneuver himself out of the corner seat where he had lodged himself. Didn't he know he was going to get off? Jasmin wondered why there were so many people on the bus in the first place. It was weird because lots of cars were still on the street, blowing horns at each other and making traffic hellacious. As many times as the bus paused in traffic, she thought that they would never move.

Like the passenger who pulled the string, she tried to make her way through the gauntlet of passengers with Stephen following close by. Jasmin looked at the passengers and felt for the fanny pack, making sure that it was still there. Last thing she wanted was to be stranded without a way back home. Plus, what if she did find Noemi? She'd need the money to get them all home. What if she did find Noemi? She thought about that again. A smile warmed her face. What if she did find Noemi? She had so many questions. *Why'd you do it? Why didn't you come home? What about Ma? Me?*

"This doesn't look safe, Jaz." Stephen's eyes darted around looking at the buildings with few strangers walking around; people like he and Jaz who should probably be at school or at work.

"Ya'll lost?" A tall guy with a deeper voice than Stephen asked. The red handkerchief tied around his head matched his red t-shirt and bright red sneakers. Like every teenage boy Jasmin's ever seen, except for Stephen, this guy's jeans rested just below his hip, revealing his red checkered underwear too.

"Naw," Stephen deepened his voice to match his. "We good bruh."

They both hastened their steps in the hopes of not continuing the conversation.

Once out of his earshot, Jasmin laughed, "bruh?"

"Yeah," Stephen answered. "Our chances of surviving are higher if we blend in."

"Right," Jasmin agreed. She stared at each one of the houses, each looking like the other and began to wonder which one was the right one. Each identical house confused her, making her wonder if she'd made a mistake. Did she need to leave this to the detective and the sergeant or was she doing the right thing?

The walk seemed longer than she anticipated. None of the houses gave her that feeling she got the first time she visited.

"I'm hungry, Jaz," Stephen complained. "We've been out here all day; even the sun is gone." Stephen was right, the sun had long left its nest and made way for the moon to begin to shine.

"I know," Jasmin agreed. "We're so close though."

"You sure? Cause I feel like we passed that same Burger King like three times already." Stephen pointed to the Burger King across the street.

"I'm sure," Jasmin answered, annoyed. "I know it's got to be around here somewhere."

Jasmin looked at the night's sky. Certain with Ma's grief, she wasn't going to even realize she was gone. Lately, she wasn't realizing a thing, not even the fact that Jasmin was present and accounted for.

Then

Noemi walked in and casually tossed her small bag on the couch, almost hitting the guy sprawled out on top of it, "Hey, Charlie, didn't see you there."

Right. Jasmin thought. There was no way anyone could miss him, sprawled out on top of the couch the way he was. With one hand inside a bag of Cheetos, the puffy ones, not the skinny ones, and the other clicking on his game remote, no one was going to not notice him. The loud smacks he made when chewing on the puffs were enough to wake a sleeping bear.

"What's up, Nome?" One by one, he licked the orange dust off his fingers making a disgusting smacking sound after releasing each finger from his lips.

Nome? Had Noemi been there before? Jasmin wondered.

"I told you not to just throw your things anywhere," Bakari barked at Noemi. "Pick it up."

"Sorry," Noemi apologized, quickly picking up the bag to place on the floor between the end table and the couch.

What are you doing? Jasmin mouthed to Noemi. Both girls had been told several times by Ma that putting your bag on the floor like that meant only one thing. *You wanna be broke?* Jasmin mouthed.

Noemi rolled her eyes at Jasmin and continued to follow Bakari up the stairs until she disappeared from Jasmin's sight. Jasmin wanted to call out to her, ask her what to do. Follow them?

She tried her best not to be this *little girl* Noemi always accused her of being. She wasn't that much younger than Noemi. They were both high schoolers, so Jasmin never understood why she insisted on calling her that, *little girl*. Jasmin could hear Noemi's voice calling her that little girl because she felt scared and worried. Strange situations made her nervous. Strange people made her nervous. Strange houses made her nervous.

Her eyes greedily darted around the room looking for a telephone but found nothing. Another exit maybe? Another thing that Ma always told them to look for in any building they entered, but she saw nothing. There couldn't be just one exit. *No way*, she thought. She knew this was not right. Everything about this. Where were they? How had they gotten there? What were they doing there? At least, what Noemi was doing wasn't right. All of it. None of it was right. Jasmin panicked, her chest tightened again, on which that elephant sat firmly getting ready to crush her, turning her lungs into mashed lungs. *One. two.* She began to count. *One. Two.* She calmed herself and tried to control her breathing.

"Lil' mama," Charlie's voice jarred Jasmin out of her thoughts. "You good?"

No, I am not good, Jasmin thought. *Nothing's good. Ma's about to get home and we won't be there. No, I am not good. We're gonna be stuck here. No. I am not good. You could be a serial killer or something. No. I am not good.*

Jasmin's feet were planted firmly on the mat that Noemi left her shoes on. *Weird*, Jasmin thought because Bakari hadn't removed his shoes and as far as she saw, Charlie, or whatever his name was, still wore his as well.

"You gonna stay there all day?" Charlie asked.

"All day?" Jasmin echoed. "We're leaving soon."

"Sure," Charlie grinned as though he knew something Jasmin didn't.

Jasmin's eyes searched the house again, at least the parts that she could see. Similar to their house, the kitchen was across from the living room where Charlie sat. Pictures of strange people lined the walls, families, individuals, fruit in a bowl. From what Jasmin could see, she had three choices: sit at the table in the kitchen, sit on the couch next to Cheeto-eating-Charlie or stand still on the mat next to Noemi's shoes until she returned. She moved towards the couch slowly.

"I don't bite, ya know," Charlie announced. "Clearly, I got stuff to eat."

Without responding, Jasmin stepped over Charlie's elongated feet to plop down on the couch, careful to leave enough space between the two. Jasmin swallowed. Her heart started beating loudly like a child going insane on a drum machine. She wondered if Charlie could hear the thump, thump, thump that reverberated in her ears. Her hands took on a life of their own and began to go up and down her thighs hoping to help calm her. *Relax.* She heard Noemi's voice in her head. *Don't be a child.*

"You nervous?" Charlie side eyed her and clickety clacked at his game.

"No," Jasmin shot back. "For what?" She steadied her hands on her thighs to keep them from shaking. It was either that or keep rubbing them up and down her thighs and she didn't think it wise to give Charlie the wrong idea.

Splashes of red periodically covered the screen as the heavily armed life-like avatar plotted its way through the war-ravaged area. Faintly, rat tat, tat, tat, sounds came from the T.V. as the avatar shot off its humongous rifle and others shot at it. Bodies dropped left and right as the avatar advanced deeper and deeper into the neighborhood.

"You look nervous," Charlie pointed out. "You ain't stopped shaking since you got here."

"I'm not shaking," Jasmin said and concentrated on staying still.

"Breathe then," Charlie chuckled. "You a little tight over there, lil' mama."

Jasmin hadn't realized but she had stopped breathing so that she could focus on being still. Her knees locked together and she hadn't even sat back on the couch to relax like her inner Noemi had suggested. She tried to ease up a bit, loosen up her body but her mind kept going back to all the scenes she'd seen on T.V. where bad things started like this. She didn't want *it* to happen to her.

"Your friend gonna be right back," Charlie pointed out. "They don't usually stay long."

"My sister," Jasmin heard herself say. "My sister."

"Um huh," Charlie said and added a handful of Cheetos to his mouth. The smacking started again. "Well, your sister gonna be right back."

"Sure," Jasmin answered. She pushed any thoughts out of her mind and forced it not to think about what Noemi was doing. She instead wondered how often Noemi came here, to this place.

"Dang," Charlie shouted and slammed the game's controller on the table.

"Aah," Jasmin gasped.

"Ain't nothing girl," Charlie pointed out. "Just the twelfth time that I've died today, no big deal."

"Doesn't sound like you're any good," Jasmin mumbled. "Doesn't look like it either." She surprised herself when the words left her mouth. Her intent was not to antagonize this stranger in these unfamiliar surroundings. Oh how she wished Noemi would return soon.

With blood gushing out of its neck, the avatar laid on the ground with its leg twitching.

"Girl, I'm good," Charlie announced proudly. "Just having a bad day is all."

"Sure," Jasmin shrugged. She hoped Noemi would return soon, sooner than the *right back* Charlie said she would.

"You wanna jump on this or nah?" Charlie nudged her with the controller.

Jasmin flinched. *Why would you give up the controller?* Jasmin thought. *This must be when the bad stuff begins. Was he going to use this as a distraction to kill me while Noemi was wherever she was? Stephen would've never given me his remote, not this easily.*

"Chill," Charlie suggested. "It's just a game."

"I don't really know how," Jasmin slowly pushed the controller away, eyeing him suspiciously.

"I got you," Charlie moved closer to Jasmin to hand her the controller.

"Umm," Jasmin swallowed hard. An extra glob of air seemed to have lodged itself in Jasmin's throat causing her to choke a little. She expelled the air from her lips and started to rub the palms of her hands up and down her thighs again. Her eyes darted around the room hoping that she'd missed some sort of exit the first time she looked. She didn't. It was still that one door in and one door out. *Wasn't that some sort of fire hazard*, she thought.

"Chill, ma," Charlie said. "It's not that kinda party."

Jasmin tried her best to relax as she held the remote. It felt like a toy in her hand, plastic and light like one of those fidget spinners that fits easily in your hand, lighter than she expected.

"Ok," she submitted. "I've never played though."

"That's cool," Charlie moved closer to Jasmin, "it's all about the movement and speed."

Jasmin nodded her head.

"So, you have to learn how to slide quick and aim just as quick."

"Ok," Jasmin nodded her head again.

"You miss one bullet and you're done,"

"Ok," Jasmin answered.

"I mean, done, done, so you have to have a steady hand and good grip on the controller," Charlie added. "Not like this flimsy soft grip you got here." Charlie held up Jasmin's hand and dropped it just as quickly. "You'll be dead in a second if you don't hold it tightly."

Jasmin gripped the controller tightly and tried her best to follow Charlie's instructions. Her avatar died several times, barely making it past one block of a war ravaged neighborhood before its head was blown off or a leg or an arm. With each injury or fatality, the screen was splattered with blood making it impossible to believe that one wasn't deeply embedded in the make-believe scenario.

"I'm getting it," exhilarated, Jasmin yelled. She sat forward, eyes locked in, fingers maneuvering the buttons so that her avatar could duck and hide, jump and shoot, flip and dive.

"Yeah," Charlie cheered. "I told you it was easy."

"Aaah," Jasmin screamed as the head of her avatar was shot cleanly off its body. Blood splattered all over the television's screen for what seemed like an annoyingly long time. "Oh, man, I thought I had it."

"Yeah," Charlie agreed. "It be like that."

"Ok, this is my last game for sure," Jasmin decided.

"Sure," Charlie said dubiously. "This is how it starts."

"What?" Jasmin asked but didn't wait for an answer. Lost in the mind of her avatar, her fingers made it leap on top of abandoned cars and reloaded magazine after magazine as she shot through the neighborhoods towards her goal. Her heart beat fast but not in a way that she needed to slow down, but in a way she hadn't felt in a long time. It was intoxicating, reminding her of that first time Ma took them to Sea World. That day, Noemi convinced her to ride Kraken. Reluctant at first, but eventually Jasmin agreed to strap herself into that roller coaster to hang upside down most of the ride. In spite of her early fear, she'd enjoyed every moment the roller coaster sped through. Playing the video game was like that. She was in control and she enjoyed every bit of the euphoric moment it provided.

"Ready," Noemi's voice came out of nowhere bursting Jasmin's imaginary rapturous bubble that floated aimlessly in the atmosphere.

"One second," Jasmin pleaded, her fingers now smoothly maneuvering the buttons on the controller, willing her avatar to do her bidding.

"No," Noemi marched around the couch and yanked the controller from Jasmin's hands.

"Hey," Jasmin protested. Her avatar immediately died a horrific death as its enemies massacred it as soon as the controller was out of Jasmin's hands.

"Let's go," Noemi demanded, yanking Jasmin's arms, pulling her up off the couch, another reason Jasmin wished she was stronger.

Really, Nome? Is what Jasmin wanted to say but instead she let Noemi lead her to the wide open door where Bakari stood waiting. He breathed a heavy sigh and impatiently tapped his heel on the mat. He was different, Jasmin noted that his demeanor was different. Impatient. But she paid more attention to the peppered stars that filled the skies. There'd been there more than a *little while*. What were they going to say to Ma when they got home?

Now

"**N**o one's in there," Stephen mumbled. His eyes darted around looking for nothing in particular but taking in everything. There was no one around, absolutely no one. No noise came from the other houses. No cars passed by.

"Someone's gotta be in there," Jasmin knocked harder this time. "I know it."

"Look Jaz, the chances of anyone being home right now are slim, less than ten percent," Stephen said confidently. "We should definitely cut our losses, go back home and call the detective."

"I'll take that chance," Jasmin answered. She held the door knob tightly in her hand. It was cold like a piece of ice before dropping it into a cup.

"What are you doing," Stephen whispered. "We can't just go in there."

Jasmin inhaled and closed her eyes, "If the door opens, we're going in. I'm going in."

"No," Stephen shook his head in disagreement.

"If it doesn't," Jasmin ignored Stephen and whispered to herself, "we go home."

Stephen did the math in his head, "Ok, it's a twenty-five percent chance of the door being unlocked."

"Where do you even get these numbers?" Jasmin rolled her eyes. She heard Noemi's voice in her head, *stop being a child*. She turned the door knob not expecting anything, but wanting everything, wanting some sort of answer. Even a *no* was better than nothing right now, better than what the detectives were giving them. It turned the 180 it was supposed to. She pushed it and the door opened like doors were supposed to.

"Oh my God," Stephen said nervously. "Who leaves their door unlocked?"

"Twenty-five percent do."

The door screamed as Jasmin pushed it open. It was just like she remembered except there was no one on the couch eating Cheetos. There were no shoes on the mat in front of the door and she thought before moving forward: should she take off her shoes or just leave them on? One foot after the other, she tiptoed hoping that, in fact, no one was home as she was now an intruder. She walked in and quietly dragged her fingers across the top of the couch. Two remotes lay idle on the center table next to a bag of half eaten Skittles.

"Jaz," Stephen whispered loudly. "Come on."

"You coming in?" Jasmin called out. "We'll just be a minute."

Stephen looked behind him, reluctantly stepped in and carefully closed the door mindful not to make a sound. He watched as Jasmin walked deeper and deeper into the house, a house that they were not invited into.

"Jaz," he begged. "Let's go for real. What if someone comes home? Whose house is this anyway?"

Jasmin ignored him and opened the door in front of her. She hadn't noticed it when she was there the last time. It was as if it appeared out of nowhere. How could she have missed this? This door creaked just as loudly as the first. Didn't they have that stuff that Uncle Dee sometimes sprayed on their door? Opening the door revealed a small bedroom much like hers except that hers was upstairs. She walked in to look around, not for anything in particular but, in fact, for everything.

"Don't go in there," Stephen silently commanded.

Jasmin did just the opposite and walked into the room. As though the bed had never been made, the checkered blue comforter was crumpled up on the bed pillows on the floor. *Ma'd kill me*, she mused. A waterfall of clothes overflowed in a hamper in the corner of the room. Loose shoes layed around as though missing their feet.

Suddenly, muffled voices and footsteps began to scrape from the outside of the house. Stephen looked at Jasmin wide eyed. "Someone's coming," he whispered.

Jasmin's eyes darted around desperately searching for a place to hide. *People get killed like this*, she thought. "The closet," she said quickly.

"Ouch," Stephen gasped as he stumbled over several shoes obstructing his path.

"Shhh," Jasmin commanded.

He scrambled in the closet behind Jasmin as the voices grew nearer.

"It's probably in my room," the voice shouted. "Gimme a sec."

Jasmin quietly and quickly pulled the closet door closed, squeezing her and Stephen into the clothes-filled coffin. Face to face, their breaths were shallow and controlled as they stood behind the row of garments that hung loosely on the rack and on top of the mountain of shoes that carpeted the closet's floor. *How many pairs of shoes does this person have*, Jasmin wondered. Through the slits of the closet door, she watched as Charlie shuffled through the crumpled-up comforter on the bed. Jasmin couldn't help but think that if he'd made his bed, it'd be easier to find whatever it is he was looking for. That's what Ma says anyway.

"It's Charlie," she mouthed to Stephen.

"So?" Stephen mouthed back, his eyes wide.

"He's harmless," Jasmin mouthed back. She was certain that Charlie would only help them. That's why she journeyed so far to this house, to this neighborhood, to find him. Had she had his contact information, even Bakari's, she would've called to find out what he knew. Had he seen Noemi? She thought about giving the detective the information as well but what were they going to do? *Look into it?* They had been *looking* into Noemi's case for some time now without discovering anything, anything that would locate Noemi. Plus, what would she have said? *I think my sister is in this house. In this neighborhood. But, I don't know for sure because it's just this feeling I have? If she's not there, they may know where she is?* Jasmin knew how it would sound so she never said anything. What was she going to tell Ma? *Sometimes me and Noemi go places you don't know about. Those times you think we're home, we're not.* She imagined Ma going ballistic after hearing this, locking them up with actual chains so that they'd be incapable of leaving the house. Home school would definitely be on board once Ma heard that! Jasmin even imagined what would happen if she reminded Ma that she went along only because she always said to stay together. She could hear Ma now, *if everyone jumps off a cliff, you gonna follow them?* But Noemi wasn't everybody. Noemi's her sister.

Stephen grabbed Jasmin's arm tightly and shook his head, no. His elbow hit the wall in the closet, making a low thumping sound.

Charlie looked up suspiciously, certain that he heard something. "Hold up," he shouted to the other room. He made his way to the closet door, now strangely closed. With his hand on the door's handle, he readied himself to open it.

Both Jasmin and Stephen could hear his breathing, loud and out of breath as though his searching took every piece of energy out of him. As Charlie pulled the door open, simultaneously, Jasmin and Stephen clapped their hands over each other's lips to stifle the screams that would most definitely be released upon their discovery.

Don't move. Don't breathe, their eyes whispered to each other. Utter terror consumed Jasmin's body. *What if Charlie found them? Was he going to be as nice as he was to her when they first met?* Questions cluttered Jasmin's mind like cotton candy squeezed into a bag. *Why'd I even come here? I should've just told the detective. Now, we're about to be killed and Ma's not gonna have nobody. Not me. Not Noemi.*

Then

"Drop us off here, please," Noemi instructed.

Bakari slowed the car, "I don't see why I can't meet your mom's."

"You will," Noemi claimed, "just not now. Not tonight."

Bakari's jaws tightened, "You gonna have to tell her sometime soon. I don't plan to wait much longer."

"I know," Noemi agreed, "I know."

Noemi got out of the car to pull the seat forward so that Jasmin could get out. Jasmin wondered why the car had to be so low. She felt like she was squatting lower than a toilet seat just to get in and out. She didn't like it, not one bit. She didn't like having to go wherever Noemi went either, but there she was, getting out of a stranger's car, something she knew she was never ever supposed to do. *I guess if I really think about it, Ma never said we shouldn't get out of stranger's cars. She said we should never get in, so was I halfway obedient?* Even while she thought about it, Jasmin knew that wouldn't fly with Ma. She wasn't going to half-way punish them because they half-way disobeyed.

As they walked on the sidewalk, making their way to their house, Jasmin asked, "What's he talking about?"

A broad frown filled her face and she began to bite her nails, something she sometimes did just before the opening of one of her plays, "Nothing."

"He wasn't talking 'bout *nothing*, Nome," Jasmin persisted, "cause you said *you know,* what's going on?"

"Nothing," Noemi answered again.

Lights streamed from the house as the girls neared. Ma's car sat in the driveway as though waiting for them to return. Both girls looked at each other.

"What are we going to do?" Jasmin asked, her eyes bulging.

"What do you mean?" Noemi responded as though she didn't know what they were about to walk into, as though she'd forgotten that they were both *where they weren't supposed to be*, as though she had more pressing things on her mind besides their pending deaths.

Jasmin swallowed hard, "Ma's home."

"I see what you see, you know?" Noemi irritatingly retorted.

Jasmin pushed her thoughts about Noemi and Bakari's conversation to the back of her mind. While she needed to find out what the two were talking about, she instead focused on how they were going to explain to Ma where they were and still live to see another day.

In the driveway, Noemi paused, exhaled, then walked forward. She then pushed her key in the keyway and hoped that the latch would unlock quietly. Before Noemi finished turning the key, Ma yanked the door open to reveal two pairs of petrified eyes.

Jasmin immediately pressed her palm against her chest and began to silently count. *One. Two. One. Two. One. Two.* Sucking the air through her nose and pushing it back through her lips was not working. She needed an actual shield, one of those things medieval knights used in battle. Or maybe she needed a knight, period. She swallowed hard hoping that Ma wasn't going to end them then and there under the innocent sky. *I'm innocent too,* Jasmin thought. But, according to the shows she watched, she was an accessory, co-conspirator. Guilty-adjacent. All of the above was not going to separate her from Noemi and the fact that they'd disobeyed Ma.

"Where were you?" Ma dragged Noemi into the house.

Jasmin dutifully followed. *One. Two. One. Two. One. Two.*

Jasmin knew it. She knew this was the night they would both die. They had been gone too long. She kept hearing Ma's voice in her head, *go where you're supposed to go and be where you're supposed to be.* They hadn't done any of those things and just like Jasmin suspected, they had been caught. Ma was going to chain them up for sure, never ever let them out again. She was going to have them looking out some window like Rapunzel. *What was Noemi going to say*, Jasmin thought. *How are we going to get out of this one*?

Ma was livid. She paced back and forth in the living room, surely wearing a path in the rug. With her hands placed firmly on her hips, she said, "I looked everywhere."

Jasmin hoped that *everywhere* didn't mean the mall because if she really did look, Ma would've seen that they weren't at the mall.

"Ma," Noemi interrupted.

"I even got Dee out there," Ma pointed. "He's out there looking for you like, like-"

"Ma," Noemi tried again.

"I got to go call him," Ma walked towards the kitchen and returned with the cordless receiver.

"Ma," Noemi explained. "We're ok."

"I can see that now," Ma looked at the phone in her hand then placed it on the center table as though she had forgotten what she was just about to do. "But where were you? Why are you coming home this late? I want you home before the sun quits. The sun out there working now?"

This wasn't one of the questions that Ma wanted an answer to and both the girls knew it.

"Ma," Noemi tried to begin.

"This is why?" Ma continued, "this is why you should just stay home. No more malls. No more nothing. Just school and-"

"Ma," Noemi belted out. "Just listen."

This should be good, Jasmin thought.

"Listen to what?" Ma paced again. "I came home and you weren't here. You weren't in your rooms. You weren't anywhere."

"But, Ma," Noemi tried.

"I don't understand why you don't do what I say, when I say it," Ma ranted.

Both girls stayed silent as car lights streamed through the house.

"What if," Ma paused and rubbed her forehead. "What if someone took you?"

"Don't nobody want us," Jasmin heard herself say.

"They're home?" Dee burst through the door.

"They're right here," Ma pointed out. "Talking 'bout they're ok,"

"But, Ma," Noemi said again, "you won't even let me explain. We weren't in any danger."

"Danger?" Ma yelled, "How do you know you weren't in any danger?"

"Hear them out, Grace," Dee suggested.

"Thank you, Uncle Dee."

"No, thank-you-Uncle-Dee, nothing," Ma answered, "be where you're supposed to be when you're supposed to be there. They were supposed to be home, and they weren't. We've looked under every crook and nanny and didn't find them. What could they possibly say about that?"

Nook and cranny? Jasmin wanted to say but held her tongue.

"We won't know til we listen, right?" Dee said softly.

Ma thought about what Dee said for a moment. She then sat on the couch, crossed one of her legs over the other, and waved her hand, "Go ahead."

Noemi breathed, "Ma, this wasn't even our fault,"

"We're way past fault and blame-"

"Let her finish," Uncle Dee implored. This was the first that he had come to the girls' rescue and neither understood that but they needed and accepted it.

"Thanks, Uncle Dee," Noemi said.

"Stop thanking him and get on with it," Ma complained.

"You know how you're always saying you want us to be more cultured?"

"Yeah, but what does that have to do with the cost of eggs?"

"Well," Noemi continued, "there was a troupe in the mall when we got out the movies and me and Jasmin stayed to watch. Jasmin didn't want to, but I begged her."

"Ok? Cause it's still late," Ma switched her legs impatiently.

"But then, they started doing improv, you know," Noemi kept her eyes on Ma making sure not to blink. "They asked people from the audience to participate. Right Jaz?"

"Yeah," Jasmin answered reluctantly.

"I didn't want to go up there at first, but then I was like, I do this all the time, so why not, right?" Noemi continued, "Well, I went up and I was good. I was goooood, Ma. Right, Jaz?"

Jasmin wished she hadn't dragged her into this, but there she was, being a co-conspirator. An accessory. Guilty-adjacent. "Yeah," Jasmin finally answered. "She was good."

"And then we sat and ate with them in the food court. I learned so much, Ma. We didn't even realize what time it was. Nobody rushed us out of the mall or nothing. They just let us sit there and eat and talk. One of them even gave me information to join their theater group, Ma. They said I could join. I'm not too young or nothing and it's not gonna cost you nothing." Noemi patted her pockets, then dug both her hands into them, and pulled out the insides as though she was searching for something.

"What you looking for?" Dee asked.

"Jaz," Noemi asked, "you got them?"

Jasmin wondered what Noemi was talking about. They hadn't discussed a story. She didn't know what to go along with, what she had to add or nothing. Now, Noemi wanted her to ad lib, concoct a story without preparation? She wasn't a third of the story teller Noemi was and they both knew it. "No," Jasmin submitted and hoped that she'd given the correct answer.

"Oh, man," Noemi whined. "I must've left the paper work on the table. Dang."

"Watch your mouth," Ma shot back. "This doesn't sound right. It still doesn't explain the time. It doesn't explain why you are so late."

"We got carried away, that's all. I was just listening to all the stories. I didn't even know that you can travel from place to place to perform. I just thought about New York and Hollywood, you know?" Noemi explained. "But they were telling us about all these different places." Childlike wonderment filled Noemi's eyes, "They even showed us pictures and showed us where we could follow them on Instagram, but we told them we didn't have no phone."

"Hmm," Uncle Dee grunted. "I told you that you need to give them girls a phone cause we could've tracked them all by now."

"Next time," Ma stood up. "You tell them people you got to go home. We were scared half to death."

Now

"Yo," a male voice shouted into the room.

Charlie jerked at the closet's door.

"Here go the remote right here," the voice said. "Let's go."

"Where'd you find that?" Charlie turned towards him and asked, haphazardly forgetting that he'd heard a noise in the closet that he wanted to investigate. "I looked everywhere."

"It doesn't matter, man, let's just go," the voice suggested. "We're already late."

Jasmin hadn't heard the other voice before and wondered who it could possibly be. *I don't really know a thing about these people,* Jasmin thought. *I know his name is Bakari, but Bakari what? Who is Charlie to Bakari?* All these things she wondered as she tried to not be detected in Charlie's-who-she-didn't-really-know closet. *But he was nice,* she remembered. *Surely, he'd want to help find Noemi too, right?*

Charlie let go of the door and walked away with the voice that Jasmin didn't know. They could breathe again. Both she and Stephen carefully and quietly released a breath so that no sound traveled through the slits of the closet door and back out to Charlie. Regardless of how *friendly* Charlie was, Jasmin didn't know how *friendly* he'd still be if she was discovered.

Don't move, Stephen mouthed.

With moving only getting them in trouble, Jasmin was ok with not moving. She was ok with not breathing, not for too long though. She began to wonder about which would be worse, Charlie finding them in his closet or Ma finding out that she was where she was. She was definitely not "where she was supposed to be and when she was supposed to be there." Charlie didn't seem like the killer-type. He didn't seem like the type of person who'd be upset at people hiding in his closet. But, then again, what did Jasmin really know about Charlie? Plus, none of this stuff was normal. None of it. Not the closet. Not Noemi being gone. Not Ma acting like she was. Not Jasmin and Stephen in a stranger's closet facing each other like they were looking into a mirror. None of it was normal. Jasmin wanted so badly to go back to normal, go back to Noemi ignoring her. Go back to school and people not staring at her. She wanted all that back, but instead, she was stuck in a closet hoping that she wouldn't end up on the news.

"That was scary," Jasmin gasped.

"You think?" Stephen said and peered out the closet, "This is our chance."

"Oh my God," Jasmin said breathlessly. "I thought he was going to see us for sure."

"He didn't," Stephen announced. "So, let's go. We gotta get out of here before he comes back."

"Ok," Jasmin submitted.

Jasmin didn't think that she was making the best decisions lately. Going along with whatever Noemi had planned was usually her plan too. But, she'd truly hoped that she'd find Noemi with Bakari, not like a *runaway* situation, but... maybe she'd knock on the door. Bakari'd open and Noemi would be on the couch like she'd lost track of time or something. Jasmin knew she was being unrealistic. No one could possibly *lose track* of days. But, she continued in her fantasy, thinking that once they were there, Bakari would take them home because taking that bus twice was too much for one person to take in one day. Then, once they got home, Noemi would concoct one of her stories and they'd be back to normal again.

The truth was, Jasmin didn't really know what she'd find. She just hoped, hoped that she'd get answers, anything other than: "it's still an open investigation," or "we are still following up," or even, "let us do our jobs." She knew that *this*, what they were doing wasn't safe. It hadn't turned out good for anyone on any of the T.V. shows she watched. Matter of fact, Jasmin couldn't recall a T.V. show or movie where people like her and Stephen ended up alive and well after they'd done what they just did - walking into a stranger's house, hiding in a closet, and still managing to get out. *Yeah*, she thought. It really sounded like the start of every scary movie, and those never ended up good either. Rushing out of the house while they still had legs seemed optimum right now. So, she followed Stephen who was already at the front door, opening it slowly.

He peeked out, "Coast is clear."

As they got ready to run through the door, escape, don't look back, never do anything so insane ever again, a loud thud echoed throughout the house as though a heavy object had fallen on the floor.

Jasmin stared at Stephen, her eyes wide open, "You heard that?"

"No," Stephen lied. "Let's go."

It sounded again, louder this time.

"I know you heard that," Jasmin said. "It's coming from upstairs."

"No," Stephen lied again, "we've really gotta go. This could be our last chance, Jaz."

Jasmin ignored him and rushed back into the house. Stephen quickly followed and grabbed her arm at the base of the stairs.

"Let me go," she spat.

"Jasmin," Stephen begged. "We don't know what's up there. We need to go...now!"

"I know," Jasmin said. "But I've got this feeling."

"Me too," Stephen answered. "And it's a bad feeling. Neither of us know how to conduct a proper investigation."

"I know, but..."

"Please, Jaz," Stephen pleaded, "let's go, call the police on my phone and tell them what we know."

"Which is what exactly?" Jasmin spat. "That we broke into someone's house and-"

"Technically, we didn't break in," Stephen reminded her. "The door was unlocked."

"On T.V.," Jasmin swallowed hard, "whenever something like this happens and you bring the cops back, don't nothing be here and then you look crazy. Then," she paused, "it'll really be about *us* breaking into the house."

"This is not T.V., Jasmin!" Stephen announced, "this is real life. Our lives. If these people find us here, there's no telling what they'll do."

"Stop it," Jasmin demanded. "I'm going."

She jerked her arm out of Stephen's grip and took the stairs one at a time. The steps were steep and swirled around to the top, making them look longer than they originally seemed. Jasmin felt that elephant again, getting ready to sit on her chest to claim her breath. *One. Two.* She counted but continued to climb. At the top of the stairs, the setup was similar to theirs: couch, computer desk, and computer, except, the computer there was one of those flat back ones like they had in the media center at school. There were three white doors closed in a sort of a semicircle. *One must be where the sound was coming from,* Jasmin mused.

"You're going or not?" Stephen silently urged Jasmin from one step below her. He was already in the thick of it. Turning back was not an option for him not unless he left Jasmin alone and that he was not going to do.

Jasmin was pleased she was not alone. If they did get caught, she was glad she was with Stephen. Hopefully, even Ma, if she ever heard about this, would be glad she didn't do something so stupid on her own.

Just as Jasmin was about to whisper to Stephen, *yeah, we've come too far to go back now,* another thump filled the air. It was closer now. *Things cannot just be falling on the ground,* Jasmin thought. *It's not like there's an earthquake or something; we're in Florida.* They both looked at each other wondering if they were crazy for doing this, roaming through someone's house. They were. *Again,* Jasmin thought, *this is the kind of stuff that people get killed for. What if, though*?

She tiptoed across the carpeted floor while Stephen crept behind her like a cat burglar, their feet sinking, leaving footprints in the carpet. It was too late for her. There was no way to turn back now. It was too late for Stephen too; he will go all the way too.

Much like when they'd first entered the house, Jasmin slowly put her hand on the first knob to turn it. She looked at Stephen waiting for him to give a statistic. He shrugged his shoulders as if to say, *not now. Not here.*

With her palm gripped tightly around the knob, she flicked her wrist to turn it. Much to her chagrin, it was locked. *Probably the only locked door in the house,* she thought. She quietly rushed to the other door, turning it after hearing another thwack. It was as if each sound called them closer, like the little crumbs those kids left in the woods to find their way back. *That story didn't end well either*, Jasmin thought, but it didn't deter her from finding out what the sound was.

With Stephen right behind, she placed a palm around the knob. She turned it and it opened easily. Both their eyes bulged out of their heads as they watched Noemi's haggard body squirm around on the floor.

Then

"Quiet," Ms. Atoms' voice squeaked through the classroom. "Quiet."

Jasmin thought that it was weird that she always tried to shout when she didn't have a shouting voice. Her voice was consistently sweet and low, calming really. So, whenever she tried to yell, Jasmin invariably thought it a struggle for her, like watching people walk in shoes that were too big for them.

Seated behind the large black desk that she was forced to share with a partner who never helped, Jasmin watched as girls continued to show each other their cell phones and giggled. Unlike the others, she had her notebook and pencil ready to go. However, she wondered if she'd had a cell phone or even a laptop, would she be acting like them? Would she be giggling with those girls? Would she not pay attention as well?

The school issued a laptop to every student, except Ma didn't want her and Noemi to have one, so they didn't. Ma decided that the computer they had at home was all the technology that they needed. Never mind that they had to share it. That was basically the only thing her partner was good for, using her computer when they had a digital collaborative assignment. Anything else, she'd have to go to the media center, use the class desktop or wait until she got home to use the hunk of junk they had.

Clunky headphones completely engulfed the ears of some of the other students. Their heads bobbed up and down to whatever they listened to before Ms. Atoms roared through gritted teeth, "I said," she paused, "be quiet."

With mouths closed, every single student stared at her because she didn't raise her voice often. When she did, though, she was really serious.

"Now let's see what they got for us today," she turned up the volume on the smart board, then moved towards her desk.

The American flag danced around on the screen as though blowing in a wind that no one else could feel. "And now, let's stand for the Pledge." After students quickly muffled off the Pledge, they sat to watch the two school newscasters on the smart board.

Jasmin and the others watched Noemi on the screen. Noemi looked more like a professional, a real T.V. newscaster while her co host looked like just another kid doing the school news.

"Who's ready for Homecoming?" Noemi asked with feigned excitement after her cohost rattled off the lunch menu for the next day. Pizza again? No, thank you. Noemi sat behind a desk with a full-blown afro that emphasized the bones of her face. There wasn't a pimple in sight, unlike Jasmin, who again struggled to keep her face clear among the countless freckles. Noemi wore a crop top under a green blazer that Jasmin didn't recognize. She looked radiant as she spoke. Her cohost uncomfortably shifted around in her seat and fumbled her words.

"I sure am," her cohost awkwardly wiped the sweat that was beading up on her forehead.

"Remember to get your tickets before they're all gone," Noemi smiled. "And don't forget, for all the dress wearers, the dress doesn't make you pretty, you do!"

Jasmin marveled as Noemi gracefully navigated yet another area of her life. Just like track and theater, she elegantly filled the screen, obviously no novice. Effortlessly, she made her cohost look like an amateur as she frequently picked up where the other obviously faltered. This was something that Jasmin felt she couldn't do, be great, like Noemi. In theater, Noemi's entire presence filled the stage whether she had the starring lead or not. Or in track, whether she won or not, the way her body moved easily around the track made her the winner, no matter what. The broadcast was just another way Jasmin and the rest of the school could see Noemi's talents.

"And now for the weather," the co host said.

"Isn't that your sister?" Jasmin's partner asked.

"Yeah," Jasmin answered reluctantly. She wasn't sure anyone even knew that they were related, except for Stephen. They didn't look alike. They had nothing that really announced that they were in any way related. So, how would she know?

"I love how she's so positive all the time," Jasmin's partner remarked. "You're so lucky."

Lucky. Positive, Jasmin thought. *Yeah, I'm lucky.* Jasmin nodded her head, not really giving an answer. This was clearly not the Noemi Jasmin knew. This wasn't the girl who called Stephen, Step-hen or the girl who lied constantly, only caring about herself. No, the Noemi everyone knew was not the Noemi Jasmin knew.

"All right," Ms. Atoms' voice broke into Jasmin's thoughts. "Let's get our day started."

Most of the students groaned, except Jasmin.

"I know, I know," Ms. Atoms groaned as well. "How dare we come to school to try to learn?"

Classes ended and like the other car-less students, Jasmin rushed to the back entrance of the school, the entrance that they weren't supposed to officially use, but every one utilized regardless.

Stephen waited at the fence with his computer in his hand and backpack thrown over one of his shoulders.

"I'm near the end," he said to Jasmin and continued to click-clack at the laptop.

"Why do you even start a game when you know that the bell is going to ring soon?" Jasmin asked, not really expecting an answer.

"One more second," he breathed heavily as though playing a game required physical movement.

"Gotta wait for Nome anyway," Jasmin replied. "But don't take too long cause you know how she is. When she's ready, she's ready."

Most of the kids had already hustled through the unofficial exit, leaving Jasmin on the side with Stephen. She was sure Stephen had started another game in the time they had been waiting. Teachers straggled out to their cars and drove out of the unofficial exit. Jasmin wondered why they even announced that they couldn't use that opening when everyone clearly did. Another thing she probably shouldn't worry about.

"I don't want to say anything," Stephen chewed on an apple he had left over from lunch. "But the chances of Noemi actually showing up is little to none."

"You got an actual number?" Jasmin rolled her eyes and didn't wait for an answer. "She said wait here. So, I'm waiting here."

"Yeah, but it's getting late and unless we got practice or something," Stephen said. "and we don't. We should go home. I don't think she's coming."

"She is," Jasmin countered, not really believing it herself. She didn't want to believe that Noemi would leave her waiting again, especially since Noemi knew how Jasmin felt, abandoned. There was no way that Noemi was going to do that, leave her stranded, not again. "She's coming." Jasmin lowered her voice. At least she wasn't by herself. At least with Stephen, she wouldn't look so strange by herself. She was glad she had Stephen to look pathetic with.

"My computer's dying," Stephen complained.

"I know," Jasmin answered.

"I don't think she's coming," Stephen grumbled.

"I know," Jasmin finally admitted.

They waited longer than necessary. Had Noemi not asked Jasmin to wait, she would've gone already, because she had no practice, tutoring, or other reason to be on campus after classes ended.

Jasmin wanted to leave but she thought about what she would say to Ma if this was the one time Ma happened to be home after school. They'd been favored in the past where they'd either gotten home before Ma and didn't need an explanation or Noemi had concocted an elaborate web of a tale that Jasmin hoped she didn't pull her into. Inevitably, Jasmin was hauled into Noemi's spun web every time. Jasmin didn't think she had the artistry or know-how to do what Noemi did, to produce a story on a whim. What did she draw on? It's not even like Noemi read a lot so she could use one of the stories from her books. The only thing Jasmin ever saw her really reading were the scripts. Those, she studied like she was going to be quizzed.

Jasmin thought about Ma again. *Maybe I can say she was at practice and she told me to go*, Jasmin thought. *No, that wasn't going to work.* She heard Ma's voice loud and clear as though she stood right next to her, *leaving your sister behind is never an option.* This was something Ma often said to both girls. *If only Ma knew*, Jasmin thought. *If only she knew how many times Noemi left me behind.*

"What's the worst that can happen?" Jasmin whispered.

"Huh?" Stephen looked at Jasmin, confused.

"Let's go," Jasmin urged.

"You're sure?" Stephen asked. His computer had absolutely no juice left, so he was more than ready to go. But, he also knew that Jasmin going home without Noemi was going to cause a major issue for Jasmin.

"Yeah," Jasmin looked at the night sky. The moon slowly peeked its head into the left over streams of crimsons. It seemed as though they were the only ones left on campus, as not even a car sat in the small parking lot at the back of the school.

They began the short trek to the house. Jasmin hoped that Ma wasn't there, mainly because she wouldn't know what to say or even how to say it. It was too late to say "practice." Maybe not too late for rehearsals, but even so Jasmin had left Noemi behind. She knew Ma wasn't going to like whatever came out of her mouth for explanation.

Lights from the houses helped make it not so completely dark. They stuck to the sidewalks instead of the streets like other students. This was not a walking-in-the-street moment. Jasmin didn't want to risk getting hit if they even tried. They maneuvered around the occasional car that hung out of its driveway but, for the most part, the sidewalk belonged to them.

From a short distance, the sound of a car grew louder and more distinct. Although it sounded faintly familiar, Jasmin paid it no mind because Noemi said to meet her at the exit, at school, no other place. So, she kept walking near Stephen. She knew better than to make eye contact with a car and its likely tinted windows.

The sound of the car became more intense as though a heart beating directly inside of her eardrums. Buh. Dum. Buh. Dum.

"At least 10 million adults, by age 70, lose their hearing from loud noises," Stephen mentioned.

"I didn't know that," Jasmin uninterestedly answered.

"I mean," Stephen continued. "I know we're not adults but we are under 70, you know."

"I am, at least," Jasmin joked, trying to ease her worry about what would happen with Ma.

A dark, black car wedged itself next to the sidewalk a few feet in front of Stephen and Jasmin. Its headlights casted a blinding light illuminating the concrete in front of them, penetrating every corner of the surrounding darkness.

"Rude," Stephen said quietly.

They both carefully walked past the car, picking their way thoughtfully. As far as Jasmin knew, this was still dangerous. Although she wasn't alone, they could still be in danger. So, she paid close attention as she tried to walk ahead.

"Jaz," a familiar voice cried. "Get in."

Jasmin turned around only to see Noemi's pony-tailed mane sticking out of the car's passenger side window.

Now

They both stood in awe, taking in their surroundings. The disheveled bedroom was a chaotic mess, clothes, papers, whatever strewn around the room. The bed, barely visible under the crumpled sheets and blankets, looked as though it hadn't been made in weeks. Pillows laid askew, and there were dark stains marring the rugged floor. The walls were dull and dingy, with marks and scuffs from careless movements. The small desk that sat by the window was a clutter with a tangle of cords, books, empty food containers, and an overflowing ashtray. The closet door partially opened, revealed a jumbled mess of clothes, shoes, and accessories both hanging on racks and strewn on the floor. Boxes of what Jasmin hoped were shoes, lined the back wall of the closet. Piles of laundry were stacked in every corner of the room, while other articles laid scattered about, adding to the mess. Several pieces of black construction paper were pieced together on the window pane like a puzzle, hindering the natural light that undoubtedly failed to fill the room. Curtains were crumpled to the ground under the window sill still attached to the curtain rod. *Did Noemi pull them down?* Jasmin wondered.

"You're just gonna stare at me?" Noemi laid on the floor barely breathing. Her hair was unkempt and tangled having not been combed in days. Strands stuck to the side of her face with dried blood. Bruised in several places, her face looked tattered. Dark circles surrounded her eyes like a racoon's. One of the spaghetti straps on her once-white tank top was broken, hanging loosely on her chest. The other tried its best to do the job of both straps. Bruises riddled her shoulders and her chest.

Frozen, Jasmin's feet felt like they were rooted to the floor, refusing to give way. *One. Two. One. Two.* She breathed in hopes that what she was seeing wasn't real. It couldn't be. This couldn't be Noemi on this floor like this. No way. This only happened on T.V.

Stephen was also dumbfounded. With his lips gaping, he too felt as though they were in some sort of a movie, one of his games perhaps.

"Jasmin," Noemi pleaded. "Ple-." The word barely left her lips before she collapsed.

Jasmin woke up from her stupor and rushed to Noemi's side. She grabbed Noemi's shoulders to help her up from the floor.

"Ow," Noemi groaned.

"Oh, Noemi," Jasmin apologized. "But I gotta help you up."

"Thanks," a low whimper escaped Noemi's lips. "But you gotta get that off first." Noemi slowly dragged her leg from under the bed revealing a cuffed ankle attached to a long chain that rattled with each move. It was heavy and looked more like it belonged holding an anchor.

"Oh my God," Stephen cried. "Who did this?"

Jasmin lifted the chain, a long and heavy thing that clanged loudly when it touched the ground. A leather cuff was attached to the chain to lock itself around Noemi's ankle.

"Noemi," Jasmin gasped. "How..."

"There's gotta be a key here," Stephen hurriedly searched the room, lifting papers and books from the disheveled desk.

"Look over there," Noemi weakly pointed to the closet. "He's always over there."

"Who?" Jasmin asked, "who did this to you?"

"Hurry," Noemi whispered. The dried skin adhered to her lips, so they were hard to open. "Before he comes back."

Jasmin rushed to the closet and like looking for a needle in a haystack, Jasmin scattered the clothes looking for anything like a key.

Clink. Metal connected to the rugged floor faintly.

"That's it. That's it," Noemi barely breathed.

Jasmin cleared out the rest of the clothes on the floor and held up the metal element she hoped was the key. With its flat top and twisted curving shape, it didn't look like any key Jasmin had ever seen but she rushed it over to Noemi's ankle. "I got it."

"Ok, hurry." Noemi whispered. Her breath was near gone.

Stephen steadied the leather strap that surrounded Noemi's ankle so that Jasmin could get the key in.

"It doesn't fit," Jasmin gasped. "This is not it."

"Let me," Stephen volunteered.

Jasmin gave him the key and he smoothly fit it into the little hole. Once it locked in, he twisted it.

"Aaah," Noemi yelled.

"Sorry, it's the other way," Stephen cried. "It's the other way." He turned the key counterclockwise and the cuff began to loosen revealing red bruises on Noemi's ankle.

"Oh my god," Jasmin gasped, "Noemi..."

"Please hurry," Noemi begged.

"We're trying." Stephen answered and carefully lifted Noemi's foot from the cuff. He dropped it on the floor and they frantically tried to lift her up but it was proving to be futile because she moaned with each movement.

"Can you walk?" Jasmin asked.

"Yeah," Noemi said. "Just. Need. A. Little. Help."

"We got you," Stephen said, putting her arm around his neck. "Get her other arm, Jaz."

They were both Noemi's crutches now, Stephen on one side and Jasmin on the other. Noemi's body was frail and brittle, freezing up each chance it got. She was barely able to hold on to the two of them with her own strength. There were so many questions Jasmin wanted to ask. *Who did this? Why? How could you let this happen? Why didn't she see this coming?* For as many T.V. shows and movies she's watched, there must've been some signs that she missed, something she could've picked up on. Jasmin felt ashamed. *Maybe this is my fault*, Jasmin thought. *At least Ma's going to think so.*

Out of the bedroom and at the top of the stairs, they heard voices coming from downstairs, the same downstairs they needed to use for escape. One voice was similar to the one they'd heard earlier.

"It's Charlie," Jasmin whispered. "He'll help us."

"No," Noemi said through gritted teeth. "We don't know that."

"He was so nice, though," Jasmin whispered.

"Let's go back," Noemi suggested. Her eyes welled up and defeat filled her face. "Please. Put me back. And. Run."

"No," Jasmin said a bit too loudly. "We're not doing that." If there was anything Jasmin knew, on every T.V. show, was that when you left someone and came back with the police, without fail, they'd be gone. She was not doing that, not with her sister.

"Ok, lay me back on the floor and wait until he's gone," Noemi suggested.

Voices grew louder as they moved towards the stairs. A decision had to be made.

What if? Jasmin thought. *No, that's not going to work.* She bit her lips thinking about what they could possibly do. Jasmin's eyes darted around. There was no other exit, just a hallway and more doors. No way of escaping.

"Ok," Jasmin submitted. "We'll wait in the closet until he's gone."

"No," Stephen whispered. "Let's just charge down the stairs now."

"Like this?" Jasmin looked at Noemi's frail body.

Noemi barely had the strength to argue with either of them. "We wouldn't make it."

"Ok," Stephen said hurriedly. "Back to the room. But. Quietly. And quickly."

They turned around and headed back to the bedroom, back to Noemi's cage where it seemed this, putting her back made the best sense. How long will her captors stay? *This is not a good idea*, Jasmin thought. But, she'd always listened to Noemi. *Maybe now's the time to stop.*

The creaking door echoed throughout the house when Jasmin pushed it. *Had it been this loud before*, she wondered. Carefully and quickly, they laid Noemi on the floor as though she was a delicate flower. Each part of her body groaned as her skin touched the floor. Jasmin and Stephen tried their best to maneuver Noemi to look as she was.

"The cuff," Noemi groaned. "Wrap it around my ankle."

Stephen rushed to her feet and anxiously wrapped the leather strap around Noemi's ankle, mindful not to add another bruise to it.

"Ow," Noemi whimpered.

"Careful, Stephen," Jasmin whispered.

"It's ok," Noemi murmured. "Hide in the closet. Quickly. He's coming."

Stephen and Jasmin sprinted to the closet, lodging themselves at either end. Much like the other closet, shoes were everywhere, some in boxes that lined the back of the closet and some strewn on the floor. They dragged the clothes across to hide behind the split doors in hopes of not being discovered. *Hopefully, this is quick,* Jasmin thought. Stephen tried to pull the doors together but they were obstructed by more shoes and clothes making it impossible to completely close.

"Leave it," Noemi barely lifted her head from the floor to instruct.

Jasmin put her fingers up to her ear, mimicking a phone.

Stephen shook his head, *no* and puts his finger up to his lips signaling to Jasmin to be quiet.

Footsteps reverberated near the bedroom's door. Like clockwork, Jasmin and Stephen stopped breathing since even the sounds of their breath would reveal their hiding place.

Why would he do something like this, Jasmin wondered.

"Who are you talking to?" Bakari's deep voice filled the room.

"Huh?" Noemi barely lifted her head.

"You heard me," Bakari barked.

"Nobody," Noemi whimpered.

"Liar!" Bakari charged around to the side of the bed. "I heard voices."

"Nobody," Noemi answered again, nervously.

"Nobody?" Bakari narrowed his eyes. "It don't sound like nobody up here."

"Bakari," Noemi sweetened her voice as much as her waning energy allowed. "I swear."

"You swear?" Bakari said through a tight-lipped smile. "You swear, huh."

"Who even knows I'm here?" Noemi asked, not expecting an answer. "You won't even let me call Ma."

"You don't need to call her," Bakari sat on the junk-filled bed that creaked with his weight. "She knows where you're at."

"I don't believe you," Noemi whispered.

Whack! Bakari hit Noemi across her face, developing yet another bruise. Little shiny stars filled the air as she tried to catch her bearings. Blood leaked from the corner of her lips and onto her tank top.

"Bakari," Noemi begged. "Please."

"Please, what?" His voice was callous, nothing like the boy she'd met.

"If you let me go now, I won't tell anybody." Noemi begged, "I swear."

"You swear, huh?"

"Yeah, I promise."

"What you gonna tell them 'bout this," Bakari gripped a clump of Noemi's hair in his hands forcing her to raise her head higher.

"I'll tell Ma that I ran away," Noemi opened her eyes widely to stare sheepishly at Bakari. "You'll never come up. Promise."

"Promise." Bakari laughed bitterly. "Like you promise to tell your Ma about me? Your promises are worth expired milk."

"I swear on my life," Noemi grabbed Bakari's ankle and slightly lifted herself up.

"Your life?" Bakari spat. The bed squeaked as he shifted his body forward and squeezed Noemi's lips together. "Can these things even speak the truth?"

The little that Jasmin was able to witness through the clothes and the slits was too much to bear. *Has he been torturing Noemi this whole time?* Jasmin thought.

"I promise," Noemi squeezed the words through her lips, "just let me go. Please."

Bakari pinched her lips tighter forcing Noemi to writhe in pain.

Unable to witness the unfathomable torture, Jasmin slapped her hand to her mouth after a gasp escaped.

Both Bakari's and Noemi's eyes darted towards the closet.

"I knew it," Bakari barked. "I knew you were talking to someone."

"I wasn't," Noemi pleaded. "I promise."

Noemi held on to Bakari's foot with as much energy as she could, trying to stop him from going towards the closet. With desperately pleading eyes, she begged him to stop.

Bakari jerked his foot out of Noemi's grip and marched towards the closet. With both of his arms, he separated the clothes on the rack to reveal two pairs of unfamiliar eyes.

"What the hell?" he barked.

Then

"You coming?" Both Noemi's arms hung outside the car's door.

Jasmin squinted and pretended not to know her, kept on walking. Stephen followed suit.

"You believe this?" Jasmin mumbled. "We waited and waited..."

"And waited," Stephen added.

Jasmin rolled her eyes at him, "Really?"

"Well, it's what we did," he answered.

"I know, but, look at this," Jasmin complained. "With no explanation, she just rolls up in some car blasting loud music. We're supposed to just get in there without questions? No. Without answers?"

Stephen shrugged his shoulders.

"She does this all the time," Jasmin complained. "And every time. Every. Time. I fall for it like a house built with cards."

"Actually," Stephen began. "If you structure the cards the right way, they won't fall at all."

"I'm so stupid," Jasmin complained.

"Stop it," Stephen commanded. "It's not stupid to have hope in people. It's certainly not stupid to love your sibling, and that's what you're doing."

"But, she's not even acting a little bit like she cares about me, the fact that I'm waiting, most of the time by myself." Jasmin continued to complain.

"Maybe this time she has a good explanation," Stephen explained.

"I doubt it," Jasmin answered. "And if she does, it's probably a lie."

Music seeped from the car as it crept behind them at a snail's pace. What should've been relief and happiness after seeing her sister, grew into frustration and annoyance. When was this going to stop? When was she going to start respecting Jasmin?

"Come on, girl, stop playing," Noemi coaxed. "Get in the car and I'll explain everything, promise."

"I don't think she wants to," Stephen pointed out.

"No one's talking to you, Step Hen." Noemi quipped. "I'm talking to my sister. My only sister. My only sibling. My little sister."

Jasmin heard every word, but none of them meant anything to her. This one, though, was unexpected. Waiting after school meant *after school*. There was nothing to misconstrue, nothing to misunderstand. Noemi asked Jasmin to wait so she waited. The sun had already quit for the day and she still waited hoping for Noemi. "She said." She said she wasn't going to do it again. Didn't her words mean anything? Why would Noemi keep doing this?

"Your little sister?" Jasmin spat, frustration filled her voice. "So what!"

"Jaz," Noemi crooned, "I couldn't help it. This was reaaaalllly unavoidable."

"Right," Jasmin agreed sarcastically.

"For real," Noemi got out of the car to follow Jasmin.

"Right," Jasmin answered again. "Just like all the other times, right?"

"Jaz," Noemi's voice softened. "I really couldn't help it."

"Sure," Jasmin answered sneeringly. "Sure, you couldn't."

"You think I want my little sister out here with..." Noemi glimpsed at Stephen. "You think I want my little sister out here alone? What kind of a person would I be if..."

"The kind of person who leaves their little sister out here," Jasmin interrupted. "Alone."

"Jaz," Noemi begged. "Come on, I'll tell you exactly what happened when we get home, but we gotta get home before Ma."

"Now you care?" Jasmin asked. "Ma's probably home and now both of us will get into trouble for what *you* did."

"Jaz, for real," Noemi pleaded. "I really intended to be gone only a minute. I didn't think it'd take that long. Promise."

Jasmin continued to walk as Noemi, Stephen, and the car followed behind.

"I'm not going in that thing," Jasmin protested. "No way, no how."

"Ok," Noemi submitted. "See you at home then. Or maybe it is the last time you'll see me since Ma'll kill me if I walk in without you."

"Noemi," Jasmin stopped and pointed out. "I. Am. Not. Going. In. That. Car. With. You."

"Ok, then," Noemi answered. "No problem at all."

Jasmin and Stephen watched as she walked towards the car. The car stopped as Noemi leaned into the window of the passenger side and said something that neither Jasmin nor Stephen heard. They watched as Noemi exchanged words with the faceless driver. Jasmin wondered how they could see out the tinted window in order to drive.

Jasmin moved closer to the car, just in time to hear Noemi say, "Please, just this once, I have to do this..."

What was she talking about? Jasmin wondered. *Who was she talking to*, this mystery person neither Jasmin nor Stephen knew. Another person they wouldn't be able to say they saw her with. Better still, the less she knew, the less she'd have to confess to Ma.

Jasmin pretended not to have been eavesdropping when Noemi returned to her side. The car and all of its noise peeled off, leaving them on the sidewalk.

"See?" Noemi pointed out. "I did *that* for you."

"Hmm," the sound inadvertently left Stephen's lips.

"Did you have something to say, Step Hen?" Noemi snarled at Stephen.

"No," Stephen answered.

"I thought so." Noemi quipped, "because this does not concern you."

"Actually, it does," Jasmin surprised herself by snapping back. "He was at school. With me. The whole time. Which is more than I can say for you, Nome."

"Where else was he going to be?" Noemi asked the rhetorical question knowing that Stephen was always at school, no matter what.

"He has stuff to do too," Jasmin defended Stephen. "I have stuff to do too."

"Right," Noemi answered.

The sidewalk curved into their neighborhood. Lights streamed from most of the houses including theirs.

"Great," Jasmin whined. "Ma's home."

"Jasmin," Noemi stopped and grabbed both her shoulders, forcing her to stop too. Stephen stopped as well. There was no way he was going to leave after waiting all that time with Jasmin.

"I am really, really sorry." Noemi said sincerely. "I know it doesn't seem like it, but I am. I really didn't mean for this to happen. I'd planned to get back to school before it even ended, that's why I asked you to wait."

"Wait," Jasmin gasped. "So you didn't go to school today?"

"That's not the point," Noemi deflected.

"But I saw you," Jasmin said confused. "We saw you go the way you always go."

"Focus, Jasmin," Noemi demanded.

"You saw her right?" Jasmin directed this question to Stephen. Quickly, he nodded in agreement.

"Jasmin," Noemi tried to get her to focus, "Do you hear me? I'm sorry. Really."

"So, you're cutting school now?" Jasmin asked.

"Oh. My. God." Noemi exclaimed in frustration. "I swear this is the last time I'm ever apologizing."

"She's sorry," Jasmin said to Stephen.

Stephen nodded his head easily, careful not to intervene.

"Is this a sorry for tonight?" Jasmin asked no one in particular.

Stephen shrugged his shoulders.

"A sorry for all the other times?"

Stephen shrugged his shoulders again.

"I don't know either Stephen," Jasmin said. "I don't know either."

After the girls stopped at their house, Stephen continued on to his.

What were they going to say to Ma, Jasmin wondered. *What could they say?*

Now

Bakari's massive body towered over Stephen's and Jasmin's as both pairs of eyes stared wide open. Jasmin's legs froze as she thought about ways in which she and Stephen could escape, escape but still help Noemi. Lead-like legs were trapped in quicksand. *We should've run like Noemi suggested, but where?* she thought. Where could they have gone? They didn't know the house. Was there even another exit upstairs? A window maybe? She'd never been in this situation before. She'd been in a closet before of course, who hadn't? Who hadn't hidden in their closet playing hide and seek or just sat in their closet pretending that they didn't hear their sister calling? Not once did she think she'd have to devise a plan to escape a closet. She tried to think of every show, every movie where this scenario had happened. *Nothing good,* she thought. *Not one of those people made it out alive.* She began to think that she should've listened to Stephen after all. *If I never see another closet in my entire life, it'll be too soon,* Jasmin thought, *if I get out of here.*

"This is interesting," Bakari smirked.

"Leave them alone," Noemi yelped. "Please."

"Who do we have here?" Bakari grabbed them both at their shirt necks, dragging them from the closet.

"Let me go," Jasmin squirmed.

"Ugh," Stephen groaned.

"You look familiar," Bakari stared down at Jasmin, "but you, you're new."

Shoe boxes fell to the ground as Jasmin and Stephen twisted and turned violently, trying to free themselves. But, then what? Where could they run? Bakari's grip was tight before he released them, pushing them both to the floor to join Noemi.

"I told you to run," Noemi faintly whispered. "You don't ever listen."

Jasmin stared up at Bakari wondering why this was happening? "Let us go," she shouted again.

"I knew you had some spark in you," Bakari grinned. "All this time, just sitting there quiet, like a church mouse."

"They don't have anything to do with this," Noemi pleaded. "Please..."

"They are in my house," Bakari roared. "I'm not in there's. You wouldn't even invite me in, remember?"

Stephen looked at Jasmin as if to say *he wasn't wrong*. But what right did he have to chain Noemi? And now, she and Stephen. Were they going to be chained up too?

"Police are on their way," Jasmin threatened. "Everyone knows we're here."

"Sure they are," Bakari cuffed his palm to his ear pretending to listen for sirens. "I don't hear nothing?"

"They are," Jasmin threatened again, "I'm not playing."

Bakari smiled and moved in closer to the three people on his floor. "Now, what am I going to do with the three of you?"

Jasmin looked around searching for anything, anything to possibly hurt him long enough for at least one of them to escape through the door and down the stairs. Only shoes, there was nothing else. No weapons. No nothing.

Think, Jasmin told herself. WWBD?- What Would Benson Do? *Use what's in front of you, that's what she'd do.* With a burst of energy, Jasmin lunged, opening her mouth as wide as she could, sinking all of her teeth deep into Bakari's ankle. His blood ran down her mouth as she spat out a chunk of skin and flesh falling on the floor like a bloody piece of cotton candy.

"You little," he barked and fell to the ground with a heavy thud.

"Run," Jasmin screamed, "Run, Stephen!"

Stephen struggled off the floor for the door.

Bakari grabbed his leg dragging Stephen back onto the floor, joining him. Jasmin climbed on top of Bakari's long body, sinking every one of her fingernails into his back. With all the energy she could muster, she raked her nails down his back creating bloody craters in their wake. Bakari screamed out, recoiled, and bucked like a feral horse but Jasmin desperately grabbed his neck to keep from falling.

"Ow," Bakari yelped.

Jasmin didn't let up. If she was going to die today, she was going to go down fighting. Fueled by adrenaline, again, Jasmin sank her teeth into Bakari, into his shoulder this time, taking a mouthful of his shirt with some of his skin. Frantically, she spat blood and cloth out and bit again, several times in quick sweeping motions.

Bakari finally dragged Jasmin by her shoulder, pulling her off of him the way one pulls a rabid monkey off of them, violent and quick.

Whack, Jasmin's shoulder hit the wall as she landed. Disoriented, she shook her head, to try to focus on the scene. Instinctually, she pounced on Bakari again as he tried to get up to find his footing. Jasmin leaped onto his wide back with a thud making him lose his balance, and Bakari staggered to the floor.

"Call the police," Jasmin shouted to Stephen, "call them now,"

Stephen reached into his pocket for his cell phone.

Whack, Bakari forced himself up with Jasmin still clinging to his back, spun around and knocked the phone out of Stephen's hand. It landed a few feet from Noemi's haggard body.

"Get it," Jasmin yelled. "Get it."

Bakari twisted his body, flinging Jasmin onto the floor, but she somehow landed on both feet with cat-like reflexes. Immediately, she threw her arms as though they were the blades of a windmill, knocking Bakari every few seconds.

"Enough," Bakari roared, grabbing Jasmin's arms and pulling them tightly into her, creating a lock.

"Let me go," Jasmin yanked. She squirmed and squiggled but with each movement, she seemed to lock herself in more tightly.

"Help, please," Noemi whispered into the phone with as much energy as she had left, "please, help. My name is Noemi Hobson, and I've been kidnapped."

Then

With Ma's car in the driveway, Jasmin's chest tightened. She felt like her lungs were about to cave in and quit. They were out way too late, especially for a school night. No one had told Ma where they were going and how long they'd be there. Jasmin knew Ma was going to be mad and eventually fed up.

Noemi used her key to open the door and they both walked in. Ma's body lay partially hidden in the lights from the T.V., absolutely motionless and quiet.

"Ma?" Noemi crept into the room.

The remote teetered on the edge of Ma's open palm as she laid on the couch.

"Ma?" Noemi called again.

"Huh?" Groggily, Ma answered.

"You fell asleep," Noemi pointed out.

"Oh, man," Ma complained. "I wanted to see what happened to him."

"Yeah, it's done, Ma," Noemi looked at *Dateline*'s credits crawling up the screen.

"Wait," Ma said as though she'd just discovered something. "If *Dateline* is done, that means it's late. Where are you two coming from?"

"Rehearsals," Noemi answered quickly.

"This late?" Ma raised her eyebrow suspiciously.

"Yeah," Noemi answered.

"Yes," Ma corrected her.

"It's on the calendar," Noemi ignored Ma's correction and answered. "It's been there for weeks."

It had been so long since Jasmin had looked at the calendar that she hesitated to believe Noemi. Noemi had not been keeping up with her chores on the calendar so why bother looking. Waste of time. Jasmin did both their chores and eventually ignored the calendar. She'd rather not hear Ma's complaints. So, she did it, all. Ma didn't know that though so, she hoped Noemi indeed had made the note like she said she had.

"Yes," Ma sat up and straightened herself on the couch. "But, this is way too late to be out and your sister, she must be tired. Did you eat?"

"Ms. Bitters fed us," Noemi lied.

"I'll call her in the morning," Ma announced. "If you're going to be out this late, we're going to have some sort of alternative. Maybe I can pick you up and you don't go on nights when I'm working, something like that."

"No," Noemi all but yelped at Ma, "it was just this one time, promise."

"One time?" Ma questioned. "It's been like this a few times now."

"This time, Ma," Noemi explained. "We couldn't avoid it. Plus we're so close to opening night, if that kid hadn't gotten that seizure, we would've been home a long time ago. I think it was a seizure."

"Wait, What?" Ma asked. "What kid? When did this happen? Is he all right?"

"She," Noemi began.

Jasmin reminded herself to stay absolutely still. Maybe they wouldn't even remember her.

"Who? What happened?" Ma's voice filled with concern, temporarily forgetting that they'd gotten home later.

"We were just about to run through our lines again, because, you know," Noemi paused for effect. "It's close to opening night and you know how Ms. Bitters is a perfectionist. I thought we were good. I had all my lines down. Movement and everything. Everybody else was good too, props, lighting, but we had to go over it again. One last time, she said, before we left. And it was already late. But since it was on the calendar, I knew you knew about it. I thought for a fact, we'd be home already. Anyway, just when we all took our places to do it again, she fell down and started shaking, twitching all over the floor like a fish out of water. Ma, it was so scary."

"I bet," Ma added.

"I'd never seen anything like that, you know," Noemi continued. "I thought she was playing, you know, so I continued with my lines cause I didn't want Ms. Bitters to get mad at me. Because you know how she is. If she is mad at one person, she is mad at all of us. But I kept on going, you know?"

Jasmin sat on the couch next to Ma and cupped her face in her palms.

"So, what happened?" Ma asked. "Is she all right?"

"We don't really know," Noemi's face softened. "Ms. Bitters ran to her side after she wasn't getting up. I'd never seen Ms. Bitters move so fast. Not never, Ma. Right Jaz?"

I. Do. Not. Want. To. Be. Involved. Is what Jasmin wanted to say but instead, she said dryly, "Um huh. She moved fast."

"You weren't scared?" Ma moved closer to Jasmin, wrapped her arm around her, and pulled her close.

"Very," Jasmin answered. At least that wasn't a lie. She was scared when Noemi didn't show up after school, scared when the car followed them, scared when Noemi asked them to get into the car. Jasmin was scared that Ma would eventually discover the lies, so many lies, too many for Jasmin to keep up with. So, she added some truth and said, "I'd never seen anything like it either."

"Did you know when you call the ambulance, the fire truck shows up too?" Noemi asked but didn't wait for an answer. "Well, that's what happened. I was wondering why is the fire truck showing up when the school is not on fire, but I guess the more the merrier, right? More people to help."

"Is she all right?" Ma asked again.

"I hope so," Noemi answered. "They strapped her onto a rolling bed,"

"Gurney," Ma corrected.

"Yeah, that," Noemi continued. "And they carried her away. Not the fire truck but the ambulance."

Of course, it was the ambulance, Jasmin thought. *Where would they fit a body into a firetruck?* Jasmin rolled her eyes.

Noemi stared at Jasmin intently as though to tell her *you better stop*.

"That was quite an ordeal," Ma said.

"Yeah," Noemi agreed. "We'll be alright though. They'll probably have counseling for us in the morning like they did when that student passed away."

"Why would they do that?" Jasmin asked angrily. "This girl isn't dead."

Ma squeezed Jasmin tightly, feeling what she thought was fear building. But, it was anger. Jasmin was angry that Noemi had lied again and now she'd killed a whole person who really didn't even exist in the first place. She was certain. Anger was the feeling she felt.

Ma patted the cushion next to her and Noemi plopped down. With both arms around her girls, Ma said, "Today was a long day, huh?"

"Yeah," Noemi said, exhausted.

"Most of my clients are old when they go," Ma said softly. "It's different when mortality shows its face at such a young age. I'm glad the ambulance got there in time."

"Me, too," Noemi concluded.

Afraid of losing the moment, Jasmin sat quietly as Ma's arm enfolded her. She felt safe, safer than she had waiting for Noemi and she didn't want Ma to let go.

Now

As the distant wails of police sirens grew louder, a mix of relief and anticipation overtook Jasmin. "You hear that?" Jasmin asked no one in particular. Glad that they were finally getting out of this mess, her body lightened from Bakari's hold.

"Yeah," Stephen struggled to get up. "It's the police. The police!"

Bakari released his grip around Jasmin to charge through the door, leaving the three in their disheveled mess. Blood and pieces of flesh scattered across the floor making the scene even worse than when they'd just found Noemi.

Jasmin rushed to Noemi's side, "We're going to be ok."

"Yeah," Noemi sighed shakily.

Stephen and Jasmin lifted her at the same time, using their shoulders as crutches. They managed her out the door to the top of the stairs. There were uniformed officers at the base of the stairs running straight towards them.

"Anyone else up there with you?" one asked.

"No," Jasmin answered. "But, my sister, she needs a doctor. Ambulance. Something."

Noemi's head hung low in defeat, Jasmin and Stephen by her side.

About the Author

@KITTIWRITER1

LEAH T. WILLIAMS IS a proud island girl who resides in Central Florida with her family. English Professor by night and Middle School English teacher by day, some may say teaching is her passion. She'd give all that up in a heartbeat to spend endless days on the beach relaxing with a coconut in hand. Check out her first novel, "Neither Out Far Nor In Deep," on Amazon, Barnes & Nobles, or iBooks. Follow her journey on all social media outlets @kittiwriter1.

Don't miss out!

Visit the website below and you can sign up to receive emails whenever Leah T. Williams publishes a new book. There's no charge and no obligation.

https://books2read.com/r/B-A-NKQW-ODKPC

BOOKS 2 READ

Connecting independent readers to independent writers.